JULIA ON THE GO

SWIMMING INTO TROUBLE

JULIA ON THE GO!
SWIMMING INTO TROUBLE

ANGELA AHN

ILLUSTRATED BY
JULIE KIM

tundra

Tundra Books, an imprint of Tundra Book Group, a division
of Penguin Random House of Canada Limited

*Publisher's note: This book is a work of fiction. Names, characters, places and incidents
either are the product of the author's imagination or are used fictitiously, and any
resemblance to actual persons living or dead, events, or locales is entirely coincidental.*

Library and Archives Canada Cataloguing in Publication

Title: Swimming into trouble / written by Angela Ahn ; illustrated by Julie Kim.
Names: Ahn, Angela, author. | Kim, Julie J., 1973- illustrator.
Identifiers: Canadiana (print) 20230485960 | Canadiana (ebook) 20230485979 |
ISBN 9781774881880 (hardcover) | ISBN 9781774881897 (EPUB)
Subjects: LCGFT: Novels.
Classification: LCC PS8601.H6 S85 2024 | DDC jC813/.6—dc23

Published simultaneously in the United States of America by Tundra Books of
Northern New York, an imprint of Tundra Book Group, a division of Penguin
Random House of Canada Limited

Library of Congress Control Number: 2023941275

Edited by Lynne Missen
Designed by Gigi Lau
The text was set in Source Serif Variable.

Printed in Canada

www.penguinrandomhouse.ca

1 2 3 4 5   28 27 26 25 24

Penguin
Random House
TUNDRA BOOKS

CHAPTER 1

Julia tucked her chin in tight to her chest, just like Coach Marissa had taught her. When she dove into the pool, she loved the way her fingers first broke through the surface of the water before her body followed.

The few seconds she was underwater with her arms stretched out like a torpedo were the best. When she came back up to the surface, Julia gasped for a breath of air before she sped down the lane, doing her quickest front crawl. Her feet fluttered, stirring the water behind her.

As soon as she touched the wall after finishing her eight warm-up laps, she turned and took a quick peek at lane number two. That was the middle lane and Olivia Huang always preferred it.

Julia liked lane three best because it was right next to the rope that separated the three swim team lanes from the public swim lanes. The pool was almost always busy, but the swimmers in those public lanes usually took it easy and didn't churn the water like the members of the Vipers did.

She and Olivia had jumped off the blocks at the same time, but Olivia was nowhere near her. In fact, Julia could see that Olivia had *just* touched the opposite wall.

Julia could not stop the smile that slowly spread across her face as she caught her breath. With each practice this season, she seemed to be getting faster and faster. They'd only been back for a few weeks since their summer break too. But today was the first time

2

she was a *full length* ahead of Olivia. At the end of last season, they had been the same speed. Julia felt sure that she must have grown during the summer!

Julia tracked the top of Olivia's green swim cap all the way down the lane. She watched it slice through the water as Olivia coasted in to tap the wall. After Olivia grabbed the pool's edge and took a full breath of air, she looked surprised to see Julia already hanging on to the rope lanes.

"Did you only do *six* lengths?" Olivia huffed as she adjusted her goggles. Her lenses were very dark, and Julia couldn't see the expression in Olivia's eyes.

"Nope, all eight." Julia was able to reply calmly because she had had enough time to recover.

Olivia's lips puckered. "Well, I don't want to burn myself out too fast. They're just warm-up laps. You're going out too hard."

Julia shrugged. She didn't think that there

was such a thing as trying too hard. She opened her mouth to reply, but before she could say anything else, Coach blew her whistle and warm-up was over.

The *real* practice was just getting started. Julia focused on listening to the instructions and readied herself to swim even harder.

The rest of the session flew by. The team did their usual drills. They practiced their best strokes. They practiced their weakest stroke — it was always butterfly. They did their flip turns over and over.

At the end of the training session, everybody was tired — even Julia. But Julia wasn't too tired for Splash Time. Coach Marissa always let the team have five minutes of fun just before it was time to go home.

Splash Time was the best. No stroke corrections, no stopwatches. Just time to play and do fun things. There were always lots of options in a place as big as Mountainview

Community Centre. It had *three* different pools —
a twenty-five-meter training pool (where the
Vipers swam), an extra-deep diving pool, and
a recreational pool with a lazy river, a row of
spray nozzles, ropes, and all the water toys you
could ask for.

Dripping wet, Julia walked quickly
toward the separate diving pool. Julia knew she
was never allowed to run on the pool deck —
the lifeguards made sure of that.

She watched her teammates, Olivia and
Taylor Bleiberg, dash off in the same direction.
They headed for the one-meter springboard,
doing their best fast walk that wasn't
technically running.

Julia thought about joining them but
counted all the people already in line. *One, two,
three, four, five* — then Olivia and Taylor! There
was no way she was going to wait for seven
people to dive ahead of her. With only five
minutes of free time, how could she spend
them waiting?

She thought about the rope swing, but there were too many people there too. The lazy river was also jam-packed.

She turned to face the diving pool. The deepest part of this pool was directly underneath the ten-meter platform. Anybody who dove from that height was so brave! But the other end of the

diving pool was still plenty deep and, more importantly, not crowded.

Julia launched herself into a cannonball in a corner away from the diving boards.

Through the ripples in the water, Julia spied a yellow diving brick on the pool floor. Sometimes people threw bricks or weighted rings into the water thinking they could dive and pick them up. But diving to the bottom of this pool was difficult. It was much deeper than people imagined. You had to know how to kick really hard and propel your body quickly downward, or you'd run out of air before you knew it.

Julia decided she would use her precious Splash Time to retrieve the brick and put it back with all the other equipment that the swim team — and sometimes the lifeguards — used for training. It would be fun and helpful at the same time.

Before plunging deep into the water, Julia looked over at the diving board and spotted

Olivia and Taylor in line. They held their arms in front of their chests, shivering because they were *still* waiting for their turns. They might not even get a single dive in before time was up.

Gripping the edge of the pool, Julia inhaled as deeply as she could. With one swift motion, she dove.

As she kicked and a trail of bubbles floated away behind her, something felt off. The brick was too far. She wasn't going to make it.

She couldn't really understand. Julia had done this dive so many times before! She had to turn back to the surface.

Back with her head above the water, Julia used her best eggbeater leg kicks to tread water while she tried to puzzle out what was the matter. She adjusted her swim cap. When she wore one for too long, it got too stretchy, and it wouldn't stay on her head properly. She tugged it down hard, but the cap was firmly on her head. It wasn't the problem.

With her legs still spinning around and around, she checked her goggles. They were tight, but not *too* tight. Sometimes if she pulled the straps too hard, she was left with dark circles around her eyes that made her look like a panda bear for hours afterwards. The goggles were fine.

Julia rocked her head from side to side. She swallowed hard and stretched her body to reach for the edge of the pool. Julia felt frustrated. Something was definitely wrong. It just wasn't clear exactly *what*.

Using both hands she pinched the concrete edge of the pool and placed the soles of her feet against the tiled wall. She tried to think.

She had been fine during practice. But now, it was like something in her head felt out of place. Maybe she was just a little tired.

Practice had been hard. Perhaps all she needed was a few moments of rest.

After taking a few slow breaths, Julia pushed off the wall with her feet and tried once more to reach the brick at the bottom of the pool. This time, she was forced back up to the surface by a sharp pain in her ear.

CHAPTER 2

Coach Marissa blew her whistle. It sounded like there was a bubble in it, and it made a strange gurgling noise. Julia had never heard it sound like *that* before.

"Vipers! Time to head home! Great swimming, everybody!" she bellowed as she clapped her hands. Her voice bounced around the aquatic center like a big rubber ball.

Julia tucked herself into the corner of the diving pool, with her back wedged into the corner and her arms spread out wide on top of the deck. She did not want to get out of the pool, not yet, anyway.

At nine years old, Julia was the youngest swimmer on the Vipers' junior team. She was a year younger than Olivia and Taylor, and two years younger than everybody else.

She'd started swimming lessons at Mountainview Community Centre a few years ago because she was always there anyway. Her parents' small restaurant, Sushi on the Go!, was right next to the pools. They were only separated by a large wall of glass.

At first, her mother had signed Julia up for swimming lessons just to keep her busy. It was hard for Julia to stay behind the counter every day after school, plus Saturdays, with nothing to do. But where else could she go? A lot of after-school programs were expensive, and anyway, Julia's parents had to run their café and wouldn't always be able to leave to pick her up. So staying with her parents at the community center was the only real choice.

Mom couldn't have known then that swimming was the perfect sport for Julia — but she knew it now.

Coach Marissa had noticed Julia swimming during these lessons. Julia had noticed the Vipers too. Sometimes, after her lesson was done, she'd stay a little and watch the team.

When Julia had almost completed her Lifesaving Society Swim for Life program, Coach Marissa said Julia should just keep on swimming — *with the Vipers!*

Julia wasn't sure at first. Of course, she had watched them swim from the deck. On days she didn't have a lesson, she'd watch them through the glass wall, but she never thought she'd be one of the team swimmers.

Mom encouraged her to join. It was great luck that Julia had found something she liked at the community center. Once she decided to join, Julia loved it and couldn't imagine her life without the swim club. She always found it hard to leave the pool at the end of practice.

The Vipers' schedule was busy. The junior team had practice after school on Tuesdays, Wednesdays, and Thursdays. Each practice was two hours. Julia didn't mind. She would swim five times a week, like the senior team, if they would let her!

Coach Marissa came up behind Julia, who still hadn't made her way out of the water. Her flip-flops smacked against the soles of her feet with every step she took.

"Julia! Splash Time is over. Go get dressed." Coach Marissa always spoke in short commands. That was Coach Marissa's style. She was like a lychee — hard and rough-looking with lots of bumps on the outside, but sweet inside.

Some of Julia's teammates scurried behind Coach, heading to the showers.

Julia frowned. She hadn't even come close to retrieving the brick. It bothered her. Splash Time had not been very splashy. Even Olivia and Taylor had both managed to dive

once before it was time to leave. Why couldn't she deep dive normally?

"I'm not asking again," Coach Marissa said firmly, squatting down to get closer to Julia.

Coach Marissa always wore shorts and the blue team T-shirt. Hers said "COACH MARISSA" across the back in big letters. Her hair, streaked with brassy highlights from years of swimming in chlorine, was always in a loose braid down her back. The whistle on a lanyard around her neck swung close to Julia's head.

"Can I just try once more? *Please?*" Julia pointed to the bottom of the pool. She turned to face Coach Marissa with her arms folded across the top deck of the pool, her chin resting on her forearms.

"Try what?"

"Diving for the brick." Now that she was talking, Julia's voice sounded different in her own head. She shook her head and stretched her jaw. It was so strange that she couldn't dive deep today. She didn't understand it at all.

Coach shook her head. "Nope. Time to shower."

It wasn't polite to keep arguing. Disappointed, Julia hauled herself out of the water and headed to the changeroom.

As she walked, she suddenly felt very hot. She pulled her swim cap and goggles off and clutched them in one hand.

With her palm, she pushed the button that turned on the shower, and she let the warm water soak into her hair. A few spots over, Olivia and Taylor were giggling as they splashed each other with water.

"I think I'm getting faster!" Olivia said, rinsing the soap out of her hair. "I wonder what my time is for the hundred-meter freestyle now."

"Not me!" Taylor laughed. "I'm still so far behind everybody during laps. My time might have gotten worse!"

"I'm going to be *so* ready for PBD," Olivia continued.

Julia perked up.

Personal Best Day, or PBD, was the most important, most serious swim day for the Vipers. For the older swimmers on the senior team, the individual times were important for rankings during the races against other clubs. But Coach always said that beating your PB was even more important for the junior team. It meant you were doing your absolute best.

Julia *always* did her absolute best, every day, but getting it timed and recorded meant it was official. They even brought out the special electronic timing equipment for this day. That's how serious it was.

"PBD? Did Coach say something about it?" Taylor asked.

"No, not *yet*." Olivia raised her eyebrows.

"Do you know something?" Taylor stopped shampooing her hair.

Julia didn't move either. She didn't want to miss a word of what Olivia was going to say next.

"I saw something on the schedule on her clipboard," Olivia hinted as she smiled smugly.

At that moment, two things about Olivia bothered Julia. First, that *look* on Olivia's face. Second, Julia didn't think it was right to go snooping on Coach's clipboard. She gave Olivia the side-eye.

"Well, when is it?" Taylor took the words right out of Julia's mouth.

"PBD is going to be next Thursday's practice!"

When shampoo dripped into Julia's eye, she put her face into the stream of water from the showerhead with only one thought — PBD was next Thursday. Julia resolved that nobody was going to be more ready for PBD than she was, especially not Olivia.

CHAPTER 3

After school the next day, Mom picked Julia up to go back to the community center, as usual. Dad could handle the cash desk *and* the sushi counter for a little while. It was better not to leave him alone for too long, though, so Mom was always in a bit of a rush.

Mom asked Julia something as they drove away from school, but Julia didn't hear the question.

"Huh?" Julia asked.

Mom raised her voice. "How was class?"

"Ms. Mendez mumbled a lot today.

Fourth-grade teachers don't speak as clearly as third-grade teachers." Julia had asked her best friend, Maricel, more than once, "What did she say?"

Once they found a spot in the big parking lot, Julia and her mother walked hand in hand down the main hallway of Mountainview Community Centre.

Julia had a little spring in her step. It was Wednesday — swim club day! She wouldn't have to spend her afternoon sitting in the corner behind the counter of the café today.

They passed the public library with people coming in and out. Then the skating rink where the Zamboni was cleaning the ice. They always played loud music while it circled around.

Looking upstairs, through a large window, Julia saw a very intense basketball game going on in one of the gymnasiums.

The community center was alive as usual.

With so many daily visitors, the sushi café, down at the far end of the building, always seemed to have customers.

Julia quickly said hello to her father, threw her backpack behind the counter and grabbed her swimming bag.

"I'm off!"

"What? No ppo ppo for Appa?" Dad put down a fresh sheet of seaweed on his board and frowned, with his bottom lip sticking out just a little too far.

"I'm too old for ppo ppos!" Julia protested. Sometimes her dad was silly. Sometimes he was embarrassing. Sometimes he was *both*.

"Just one. Quick." He crouched behind the counter, so the bottom of his apron touched the floor.

Julia rolled her eyes. "Okay, but I get to press the silly button."

She quickly gave him a kiss on the cheek, just above his big mole. Then she pressed her

finger against the mole. "Boop."

"Going up!" Dad stood up slowly while he held out both of his hands.

Somehow, he had managed to look and sound like a robot. Julia suppressed a smile.

"That silly button works well, doesn't it?" Mom laughed.

Her parents waved goodbye, and Julia headed to the aquatic center.

After changing, Julia waited on the long wooden bench that was pushed up against the wall near the rack of life jackets. From here there was a good view of the entire facility.

As she sat on the bench, she bobbed her knees up and down. There was still fifteen minutes before practice started, but Julia never minded waiting here. She adjusted her swim cap and tugged it down tight.

Just like at the end of practice yesterday, something felt a bit off. It couldn't be because she was tired. She wasn't tired at all! She pulled off her cap, retied her ponytail, put her cap back on, and rocked her neck from side to side.

When she saw that the other swimmers were starting to make their way to the pool deck, Julia decided to push the weird feeling out of her mind and started to warm up.

She threw a kickboard onto the cement floor and sat on it with her legs together. She bent over and grabbed her toes. That made her feel suddenly uncomfortable, but stretching was very important before swimming, so she told herself that it was a head rush, like that feeling of getting up too fast.

"Hey, Jules." A few of the older swimmers greeted her. Eli and Farouk were only a year or two older, but the age difference sometimes made Julia feel awkward. They were friendly, but they were not her friends.

Julia didn't really have a friend on the team. But at school, she had Maricel. Maricel made her laugh, and even though sometimes she wished Maricel liked swimming instead of dancing, Maricel always listened when Julia told her about the swim team.

Julia smiled and said hello back to the other swimmers, but she rested her face on her knees instead of talking more.

When Coach finally blew her whistle to start practice and had everybody's attention, she announced, "Next Thursday is PBD!"

All the swimmers eyed each other and murmured among themselves. Olivia flashed her know-it-all smirk again, because it wasn't news to her. "See?" She elbowed Taylor in the ribs. "I was right."

Julia didn't want to look at Olivia anymore. She focused on Coach Marissa instead.

"Swim hard today. You've only got three more practices before then!"

She motioned for everybody to line up in their lanes. With more focus than usual, the Vipers silently began to launch themselves into the pool.

When it was Julia's turn, she dove without hesitation. She ignored the uncomfortable, weird feeling she'd been having in her ear and kept swimming.

After practice, during Splash Time, Julia saw the yellow brick still sitting on the floor of the diving pool. She was determined to get that brick today.

Just like the day before, Julia took a big breath and propelled herself deep down toward the brick. And, same as yesterday, a sharp pain sent her straight back to the surface.

Julia lifted herself out of the water and shook her head. The water streamed off her, and she pulled at her earlobe, which was sticking out past her cap. Her ear hurt even more than yesterday. Now, it was hard to ignore the fact that her ear throbbed.

"What's wrong?" Coach Marissa called out to Julia.

Julia's face contorted as she tried to figure it out. She bent over.

"I think it's my ear," Julia said, pointing to the side of her head.

Concerned, Coach Marissa approached Julia. "Were you diving? Deep?" Coach glanced at the diving pool.

Julia straightened her back and nodded. She felt a bit better now that she wasn't diving.

"Were you trying to get that brick again?" Coach peered into the rippling water.

Julia nodded.

"And you couldn't get it? Just like yesterday?"

Julia gave her right earlobe another tug and nodded. She pressed her palm to the side of her head.

Coach suddenly looked worried, and after a few seconds, she glanced at her watch. She

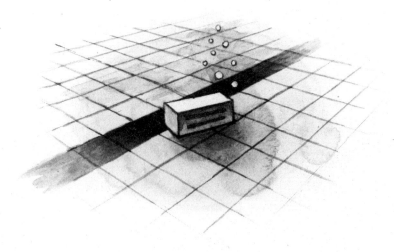

turned away from Julia and blew her whistle. "Time to go home!" she bellowed to the team.

Julia winced with the whistle blowing so loudly, so close to her. There was no arguing with Coach, or her whistle.

Coach Marissa turned back to Julia and eyed her with a curious look. Her voice softened. "When did your ear start to hurt?"

"Well, I noticed it during Splash Time yesterday. The first time I tried to dive for that brick," Julia told her, pointing down to the diving pool. "Then again today."

"So, not when we were diving in to do laps?"

Julia thought about it before she answered. "Just a little twinge, but it didn't really *hurt*."

"Hmm." Coach Marissa seemed very serious. More serious than usual.

Julia waited for her to say more.

"Go get changed. Come back and see me. We should talk to your mother," Coach Marissa ordered.

Julia looked through the large wall of glass to her parents' sushi café.

Mom was watching them. Julia waved at her, and her mother wiped her hand down the front of her apron and waved back.

"Okay, Coach," Julia replied, feeling worried. Coach Marissa never spoke to her mother. There was never any reason to.

CHAPTER 4

The wall-mounted hair dryer blew hot air over the top of Julia's head. As her hair flapped around, she jerked her head from side to side to try to get any extra water out of her ears.

"Great swimming today!" Ms. Fargas said loudly. She was making sure Julia could hear her over the noise of the hair dryers.

Ms. Fargas was one of the center's custodians. She was a small woman, and her glasses, perched on the top of her head, were usually nestled into her short, dark hair. She knew all the members of the swim team by

Vooooooo

name and always had a smile ready for everybody.

Sometimes Ms. Fargas brought homemade muffins to Julia's parents. Her parents would then offer Ms. Fargas something from the cooler in return, and she'd always say no — at first. Then Julia's parents would keep insisting. Then Ms. Fargas would say "No, thank you" again. Then Julia's parents would keep insisting, more forcefully, until Ms. Fargas finally took something home. It was always like that. Julia thought it was a strange game that adults played.

"Thank you," Julia answered. She made sure she was loud enough to be heard. She managed to smile weakly at Ms. Fargas, even though she was worried because of how Coach was acting.

The dryer turned itself off. Her hair was still very damp, but she needed to hurry. Julia hoisted her swim bag over her shoulder. Because of the wet towels, the bag was always heavier at the end of practice than it was at the start.

Coach Marissa was waiting for her, just outside the changerooms.

"Come on," she said, leading Julia to the pool's exit.

Julia followed Coach Marissa until they reached the front counter of Sushi on the Go!

Julia's mother looked surprised to see them together. But she stayed at the register until her customer finished tapping his debit card on the point-of-sale machine.

"Thank you, come again!" She handed a copy of the receipt to the customer and then wiped her hands down the front of her apron.

As Julia ducked under the counter, Mom pressed her lips tightly together. For some reason, Julia thought Mom seemed a tiny bit nervous.

"Hi, Mrs. Nam." Coach Marissa stayed on the other side of the counter.

Mom took a few quick steps toward Coach Marissa. "I'm sorry the fee is late. I promise we can pay it next week."

"Oh, of course. I'm not here about that," Coach said in a hushed voice, waving her hand and gently putting aside Mom's comment.

"Oh! Sorry, I just thought . . . Everything okay?" The nervousness slipped away from her eyes and was replaced with curiosity.

"I hope so," Coach said. "But I think it might be a good idea to get Julia's ear checked out. She was complaining about an earache when she was diving."

"Oh, I see." Mom pressed her lips together again as the corners of her eyes tensed. She glanced at Julia in a way that made Julia look away.

"I mean, it *did* hurt, just a little. But it doesn't hurt now!" Water from her shoulder-length hair start to drip and soak her hoodie. Julia wished she had dried it a little bit more. But it was true, her ear didn't ache . . . at least not anymore.

"But the point is, it *did*," Coach said gently. "Just promise me you'll get it checked out."

"Okay, we will." Mom pushed her glasses up using the back of her hand.

Julia's father had been helping a customer and came by just as Coach left.

"Something wrong?" he asked. Dad and Mom wore matching blue aprons. They thought it was cute.

"Earache."

"Oh." Dad looked thoughtful. "Remember when she had that ear infection as a baby? Actually, she had it *two* times! All that crying!"

Mom let out a small laugh and rolled her eyes. "Oh my. I haven't thought about that in a long time. I want to forget it."

Julia scowled and crossed her arms. "Why?"

"What's the word?" Mom searched her mind for the perfect word in English. "Nightmare!" she said as she opened her eyes wide and stared intently at her daughter. Julia's parents loved to tease her. Sometimes it was funny, but sometimes Julia did not like it so much.

While her parents chuckled, Julia, still frowning, reached for one of the packaged

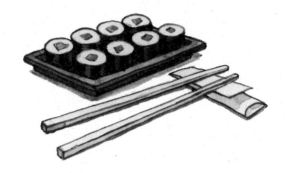

kappa rolls her father had just made. She liked simple sushi with only one filling. Cucumber-filled kappa rolls were her favorite, followed by avocado rolls, and lastly oshinko rolls with crunchy yellow pickled radish.

Julia snapped open the clear plastic container and picked up a piece with her fingers.

"Manners," Dad scolded as he passed her a pair of bamboo chopsticks. He always tried to sound strict, but he was too kind-hearted to ever look mad.

Before taking the chopsticks, Julia popped the piece into her mouth. Dad gave her a gentle click of his tongue but couldn't hide his smile.

Julia moved to sit in her usual spot. She chewed thoughtfully before swallowing. She didn't remember hearing that she'd had an ear infection as a baby, never mind *two* of them. What did Mom even mean by calling it a "nightmare"?

She pulled the chopsticks apart and picked up her second piece of kappa roll.

The line at the counter suddenly grew, and her parents were busy with more customers. Sometimes people were happy to just pick up a pre-made roll, especially if they were in a hurry, but usually they liked to order a fresh roll instead. Customers seemed to enjoy watching Dad press the sushi in the bamboo mat right in front of them.

Julia remembered when her parents had first opened Sushi on the Go! a few years ago. They had worked so hard to save enough money.

Dad had worked at other people's sushi restaurants for a long time, learning how to do things properly. Mom had worked two part-time jobs too, one at night. She was always tired when she took Julia to school in the morning. These days they still worked hard, but now they worked for themselves. Mom wasn't as tired in the mornings either.

When they first opened the café, Mom and Dad had been really shy when talking to customers, because they were nervous about their English. But now they chatted with all their regulars and even told jokes! Julia didn't *like* all the jokes, some of them were corny, but still, telling jokes in English meant that her parents were getting more comfortable with it. Nobody cared if sometimes they said things a little bit wrong.

Julia watched her mother pour miso soup into a container and press the lid down nice and tight to make sure it was spill-proof.

"I gave you extra tofu." Mom winked at Lorna, the children's librarian. Lorna loved miso soup. She especially loved extra tofu squares. Julia thought tofu tasted pretty much like squishy nothing, but everybody liked different things.

Julia wasn't supposed to tell anybody, but sometimes Lorna put aside new books for her before the other kids could read them.

Nobody could remember which had come first: Lorna saving a book for Julia, or Mom giving Lorna extra tofu.

"Julia, I have something for you." Lorna's brown eyes twinkled. Then she raised her eyebrows.

That was the sign. A new book had come in.

Julia raised her eyebrows back. "I'll come get it now," she whispered. It would be no good if other people knew what was going on. She didn't want to get Lorna in trouble.

Mom leaned over and said in a hushed voice, "No, no. Get the book tomorrow. I have to take you to the walk-in clinic before it closes." She untied her apron.

"Oh." Julia felt disappointed.

"You can handle everything?" Mom asked Dad.

He nodded. "Sure, sure. Best to check it out now."

Lorna looked concerned. "Everything okay?"

"Fine, fine," Mom said quickly as she smiled. *Too quickly*, thought Julia.

Julia knew the difference between Mom's real smile and her customer-service smile. This was definitely a customer-service smile, because the muscles around her mouth were tight and not relaxed like they were with her real smile.

"No worries, I'll be in the library tomorrow," Lorna whispered to Julia. "You can come then." Lorna picked up her bowl of soup, her California roll, and a set of chopsticks before she made her way to a nearby table.

Julia ate the last piece of kappa roll and grabbed her mother's hand. Mom squeezed extra tight. If her mother was taking her to the clinic during the dinner rush, Julia knew it must be important.

She tugged at her ear. It felt . . . sort of normal. Sometimes there was a dull ache, but sometimes it was fine. It was mostly fine! Except when she tried deep diving. But was it really so bad that they needed to leave the sushi café and go to a walk-in clinic right away? Julia wondered what was happening to her.

CHAPTER 5

Julia and her mother waited a long time to see the doctor. As she sat there, Julia read all the books in the waiting room, even the small square ones for babies. She played with a shape-sorter cube until she could do it with her eyes closed. While keeping herself busy, Julia also asked her mother every fifty-five seconds if it was their turn yet.

Finally, they called her name, but Julia didn't hear. Mom had to tap her on the shoulder.

The doctor had long black hair in a ponytail and wore a white lab coat. She adjusted the stethoscope around her neck before she patted the exam table. Julia hopped up and sat down. The paper covering the table crinkled softly. Julia read the doctor's name tag: *Dr. Deol.*

She had an angular face and very long eyelashes. In her hand, she held a black stick with a pointed end that shone a bright light into Julia's right ear. The doctor leaned closer to Julia and mumbled something.

"What did you say?" Julia asked. Dr. Deol did not speak clearly, but Julia liked the way she smelled. It reminded Julia of fresh flowers from the grocery store.

"Oh no," Mom muttered.

Next, the doctor quickly checked out Julia's left ear. "Yes, the fluid is just on the right side. This side is clear." Julia noticed that she sounded more distinct from this side.

Suddenly, it was like a picture emerging in a dot-to-dot puzzle. The time Coach's whistle sounded garbled. Ms. Mendoza not speaking clearly in class. The weird feeling in her ear.

She couldn't hear anything on her right side because there was *fluid* in her ear!

Dr. Deol reached into her pocket and took out a thermometer. She held it up to Julia's forehead, pressed a button, and then looked at the results.

"Hmm," the doctor said, followed by some more mumbling. Julia knew that when adults said *hmm* like that, it usually wasn't a good thing. It sounded the same as Coach Marissa's earlier *hmm*, before they ended up at the clinic.

The doctor moved to Julia's left side and whispered, "Can you hear me?"

Julia wrinkled her forehead. "Yes."

Dr. Deol moved to Julia's right side and mumbled something else.

"What did you say?" Julia asked. She felt a tiny little lump rise in her throat. It was official — something was wrong with her right ear.

The doctor looked at her mother, and Mom squeezed her lips tight.

"Is she in any pain?" Dr. Deol asked Mom.

Julia turned her head so her left ear was closer to the doctor.

"Only when she was diving."

"I'm a swimmer!" Julia declared.

"Do you do a lot of diving?" Dr. Deol asked Julia directly. "Deep?"

"Well . . . I *can* dive deep." Her mind went straight back to the yellow diving brick that was probably still sitting on the bottom of the pool.

"Hmm," Dr. Deol said vaguely. There was that *hmm* again. She started typing quickly on her laptop. "Because she's running a low-grade fever too, I'm giving you a prescription."

"I remember." Mom sighed. "The pink stuff."

Unlike her mother, Julia didn't remember the pink stuff at all.

"Yes. Take the full course. Don't stop. Even if everything seems fine." Dr. Deol seemed to speak only to Mom now, and Julia felt like she wasn't even there anymore.

"How many days?" Mom asked. Julia leaned in with her left ear.

"Ten."

"I can still go swimming, right?" Julia asked. Personal Best Day was next Thursday. She counted the days on her fingers and tried to match them up with the Vipers' practice days.

Dr. Deol swiveled in her seat and faced Julia. "Well, that's up to you and your family. If you do go into the water, I would just say, be really careful about diving and going too deep. This is not a swimmer's ear infection, which occurs in the outer ear canal. This is an infection in your middle ear, behind your eardrum. If you do a lot of deep dives, there's a chance the pressure will build, and then your eardrum could burst."

Julia's eyes popped open. A burst eardrum did not sound good. She pulled at her right ear. It didn't hurt *all* the time. Just once in a while. She suddenly felt a little hot. Probably because the room was stuffy.

"It's not likely to happen, though," Dr. Deol added.

"Hmm." Mom's mouth twisted. Julia was getting sick and tired of that sound.

"Is there anything I can do?" Julia begged. "Anything at all?"

Dr. Deol thought for a moment. "It's a good idea to keep the ear as dry as possible. They do make earplugs to keep water out, but I'm not sure how useful —"

"That sounds good!" Julia exclaimed. She wouldn't mind wearing earplugs for a little while if it meant she could keep swimming. She didn't want to miss practice on Tuesday or Wednesday, and especially not on Thursday!

"I think they have ones you can buy at the pharmacy or custom-made ones." Dr. Deol typed and looked intently at her screen before turning it toward Mom.

"Custom?" Mom asked. Her eyebrows wrinkled.

Julia glanced at her mother and then took a quick peek at the screen. It said: *Custom Silicone Earplugs Starting from $249.*

Mom brought her hand up to her mouth and murmured, "Oh, bissa."

Julia didn't know a lot of Korean, but she knew that that was the word for *expensive*.

"There's always the ordinary kind at the pharmacy," Dr. Deol told Mom. She lowered her voice. "I think those are a lot cheaper, but I don't have much experience with them and don't really know how effective they would be."

"Oh, if they won't work, what good are they?" Mom replied. "Even if they are cheaper. Maybe it's just like throwing money away."

Julia found it hard to argue with that.

"As I said, the most important thing is to keep the ear dry." Dr. Deol looked back at her computer screen.

"You know what is the best idea? No swimming at all," Mom said firmly. "Let's be safe! It's just ten days." She turned to the doctor and explained, "Julia can't help herself. She will dive without thinking."

Julia crossed her arms. "I can think *not* to dive!" she protested.

Mom made a face. It was clear she did not believe Julia.

"It's a choice you need to make as a family," Dr. Deol said, handing Mom the prescription.

"I choose swimming!" Julia said. "I promise, I won't dive!"

Mom's face darkened. "We'll talk at home."

Julia knew that expression. Coach Marissa and her mother had one thing in common — that face they both made when there was no arguing allowed. The only difference was that her mother didn't have a whistle. But if Mom had had a whistle, Julia knew she would have been blowing it right now.

Julia felt her shoulders sag. Ten days without swimming seemed impossible. It wasn't "just" ten days to Julia. Because during those ten days, the Vipers were going to be timed for PBD — Julia was going to miss it.

CHAPTER 6

"Yuck!" Julia smacked her lips together.

"Not so bad!" Mom claimed. She put the bottle of medicine in the fridge and pulled a box of banana milk out. She punched the straw into the small hole and passed the drink to Julia, who was sitting at the kitchen table. Julia took a big gulp.

"How do you know? You're not the one who has to have it!"

Mom smiled. "Well, I *guess* it's not so bad. The color is so pretty, like a flamingo! How can it taste bad?"

"Just because flamingos are pretty, that doesn't mean I want to eat them."

"Okay, okay. Maybe it doesn't taste good. What does it taste like?" Mom folded her arms across the kitchen table and leaned in.

"It's wet but it has a texture like powder at the same time. Gross powder." Julia smacked her lips again. "Fake-tasting gross powder."

"Well, it will make you feel better, so there's no choice."

"I know, I know. I'm taking it. But I don't have to like it." Julia guzzled the rest of her banana milk.

"Did you shower at the pool?" Mom smelled the top of Julia's head.

"No, I just dried my hair a little bit." Coach had been waiting for her. She hadn't had time.

"Take a quick shower, and then let's go pick up Appa."

"Okay, I'll be fast."

The family had only one car, and after

picking up Julia's medicine from the pharmacy, they had come home to their rental apartment.

Julia knew she wasn't old enough to stay home by herself yet, not even for a little while. They needed to go back to the café together.

"I should help you wash your hair today," Mom said as Julia headed to the bathroom.

Julia was shocked. "I'm not a baby. I can do it."

Mom looked at her very gently. "I know! You are growing up. I'll only help you *today*.

You won't be swimming for a while, so you don't have to wash chlorine out next time."

Julia's mouth puckered, and she felt little wrinkles forming on her upper lip. This ear infection was very annoying.

Mom's phone chirped. *Kakao!* It was a text message. Mom pulled her phone out of her sweater pocket. She looked at the screen and said, "Quickly. Appa is having a hard time closing the café by himself." Mom shooed Julia down the hallway.

"Okay, okay." Julia didn't want to keep Dad waiting. There was always a lot to clean up at the end of the day.

Julia went into the bathroom and waited for her mom.

When Mom finally came into the bathroom, Julia was surprised to see what she had in her hand — it was the watering can from their small balcony.

"I thought we were in a hurry. Why are you watering the plants?" Julia asked.

"I'm not."

Her mother glanced at Julia quickly and then focused on filling up the can.

"Is that for *me*?" Julia asked, suddenly realizing what might be happening.

Mom gave Julia a weak smile.

"I am not one of your tomato plants!" Julia muttered as her mother motioned for Julia to tilt her head back.

"Just trying to keep your ear dry." Mom was apologetic but didn't stop. Soon she was

right on top of Julia.

As her mother watered her, Julia felt helpless. It got even worse when Mom squeezed shampoo into her hair and started vigorously lathering it. She had surprisingly strong fingers.

"Maybe I'm being a little too worried," Mom said quietly. She gave the watering can a long look as she refilled it.

"You're telling me!" Julia felt like a big houseplant that couldn't take care of itself.

"No, no." Mom quickly changed her mind. "Better safe than sorry, I think. Let's keep your ear as dry as possible. See how I can control where the water goes! Keeps it away from your ear. Can't control water in a swimming pool."

Julia frowned slightly but remained silent. She tilted her head back and pointed her chin up to the sky so her mother could put the tip of the spout right at her hairline for another rinse.

Julia thought that there *had* to be a better way than this.

When Mom was satisfied that Julia's hair was clean, she squeezed water out of the ends and said, "Hurry, we have to get Appa."

As quickly as possible, Julia dried herself off.

So far, this ear infection had been nothing but bad news. She couldn't pick up the special book from Lorna, had to take yucky medicine, needed to be treated like a baby houseplant, and, worst of all, she was going to miss PBD. Julia was sure that things couldn't possibly get any worse!

CHAPTER 7

When they arrived back at the community center, it was much quieter than when they had left.

Usually, by seven thirty in the evening, the Nams stopped making custom rolls and sold only what was left in the cooler so they would have time to clean the café. But now, it was almost eight o'clock, the time they usually closed.

It was so late, Julia worried she was going to miss Saleema and today's Shared Meals pickup. Some days Dad made too many rolls and they didn't all sell before it was time to go home. Shared Meals made sure that the food did not go to waste.

Julia hurried so she could do her special job.

Using a permanent black marker, she wrote *Enjoy! From Sushi on the Go!* across the top of the containers of pre-made sushi that hadn't sold. She also drew a happy face. Then she put them in a bag for the Shared Meals program. Julia was ready for Saleema now.

They had been helping with Shared Meals for almost as long as they had owned the sushi café. Julia still remembered the day, not long after they had opened, when Saleema first came up to them and told them about the program. Julia's parents listened carefully to what Saleema said about people sometimes not having money for food, and how important it was for restaurants to not waste food that was still good.

Julia was surprised when her mother told

Saleema, "We had a hard time before. We know."

Julia was amazed to hear Mom talk about that hard time, because her parents never talked about it much.

Before, when Mom lost one of her part-time jobs, she took Julia on two buses to go get a box of food. Julia remembered making that trip with Mom a few times.

Julia had asked her mother why they just didn't go to the grocery store, like they used to, and Mom had said they couldn't go there for a little while.

Julia remembered standing next to her mother in a long line. It wasn't like a regular grocery store. You didn't get to pick anything or browse aisles. Someone just gave you a box. Her mother was always quiet, and she'd held Julia's hand very tightly as they slowly made their way to the front of the line. When they finally got their box, Mom always looked so happy carrying it away.

Ever since they met Saleema that first time, they saw her almost every day. Sometimes it was one of her friends, but usually at closing time, they could count on seeing somebody from Shared Meals.

Julia glanced expectantly down the long main hallway of the community center. Saleema was coming! She was wearing her bright red Shared Meals T-shirt and pulling her little handcart with an insulated box to help carry everything. Her dark curls bounced around her shoulders.

"Hey, hey, Water Rocket." Saleema greeted Julia with an open palm. Julia smacked her hand loudly, and Saleema's gold bracelets jingled. Then they closed their fists and tapped their knuckles together. Julia loved that nickname and their secret handshake. "What have you got for me today?"

"Only two leftover B.C. rolls." Julia passed Saleema the bag. "Nobody wanted smoked salmon today, I guess."

Mom and Dad were busy mopping the floor and wiping the counters, so they just waved at Saleema, and she waved back.

"Somebody will eat these very happily." Saleema put the bag in her box and closed the lid.

Julia knew she was right.

Before, when she had sometimes gone to school a little bit hungry, she had always been happy when somebody shared snacks with her. Now, when she had extra snacks, Julia made sure to share them too. That's what she and her best friend, Maricel, did — they shared.

They had known each other since first grade, but one day Maricel had heard Julia's stomach grumble and asked her if she wanted half of her sandwich. Maricel had said she wasn't especially hungry that day. From that moment, Julia knew that Maricel was the kind of person she always wanted to be around.

It was good to share when you could, especially when you had something that could make other people feel better. Not to mention,

her father's B.C. rolls were tasty. It was even better to share when the food was delicious.

"How'd swimming go today?" Saleema asked.

Julia frowned. "Fine, until my ear started to hurt. I have an ear infection."

"Oh, bummer." Saleema looked at Julia sympathetically. "I think they're pretty common. You'll get over it quickly and be back swimming before you know it."

Julia sighed. She wondered why adults always said things like that. It was frustrating!

"What's *your* favorite thing in the world?" Julia asked.

Saleema thought for a few seconds before answering. "Well, if I had to pick . . ."

"You *do*, because I just asked you."

Saleema laughed. "Okay, I'll pick! Um. . . . My favorite thing in the world is getting a cup of coffee in the morning."

"Adults and their coffee . . ." Julia moaned.

"It's delicious!" Dad chirped, lifting his coffee cup in the air.

"I agree, Mr. Nam!" Saleema laughed with Dad.

Julia said to Saleema, "Imagine if you couldn't have *coffee* for ten days, just like I can't swim for ten days!"

Saleema looked at Julia thoughtfully. "Ten days with no coffee. Oh." She seemed to be thinking. "You're right. That would be tough. Missing swimming will be hard."

Finally! Somebody saw things Julia's way. "Really hard!"

"*But* you can get through it."

"Sure. I guess," Julia said, shrugging her shoulders. She knew she *could*, it was just that she didn't *want* to. "But I'm also going to miss PBD."

"Now, I don't know what PBD is, but I'm a firm believer in rolling with it."

Julia scrunched her nose. "Is that why you're always pulling a cart?"

"That's a good one!" Dad laughed from behind the counter.

Saleema let out a big belly laugh too. "No, it's an expression!"

Julia hadn't *meant* to be funny. She wasn't sure why everybody was laughing. Her nose felt permanently wrinkled. "What does it mean?"

"Sometimes, things happen for a reason, or maybe for no reason at all." Saleema grinned. "I think the key is how you handle unexpected things thrown your way. That's *rolling with it*."

Julia frowned.

Saleema added quickly, "But I know right now that it just kind of *stinks,* and it's hard to see the big picture."

"It doesn't just stink, it reeks," Julia replied. "I don't like this big picture at all."

Saleema smiled at Julia before she glanced at the time on her phone. "I've got to get going. Need to collect as much food as I can. There are hungry people waiting. See you tomorrow."

"Bye." Julia waved.

Saleema headed to the coffee shop at the other end of the community center for another pickup, pulling her cart behind her.

Dad draped a large piece of cloth over the cooler and started to pull the metal gate around the counter of Sushi on the Go! It was finally time to go home.

Giving the pool one last look, Julia stared wistfully at the people still swimming. For the next ten days, she would not be one of them. No matter what Saleema said, she wasn't sure she could *roll* with the idea of missing swimming at all.

CHAPTER 8

During school on Thursday, Julia found it hard not to think about the practice she was going to miss later that day. She wasn't even feeling bad. The medicine must have started to work. She couldn't see why she needed to miss any swimming at all.

Later, just before four o'clock, Julia had her nose pressed up to the glass wall behind Sushi on the Go! She watched the team — her team — gather on the pool deck. When the glass started to fog up, she wiped it down.

"Come away," Dad urged.

Julia didn't step back immediately. She couldn't just yet. She frowned as she saw the team do all the usual stretches without her. Her stomach twisted into little knots when she watched them dive into the water to start their laps.

Why couldn't she be practicing with them? Wasn't there a way to keep her ear dry *and* swim at the same time? She felt sure that, if she thought long enough about it, there *must* be a way for her to get back into the water sooner than nine days from now.

When the whole team had entered the water, finally, Julia walked away. Watching the team swim without her didn't feel good. In fact, it made her feel downright sad. Maybe even a little angry. And a whole lot frustrated.

Unhappily, Julia plunked herself down in her usual spot. But she was *so* bored just sitting on the stool. She slouched, her back pressed up against the glass wall, and crossed her arms.

Something caught her eye. Her swim bag from yesterday was still sitting there. With all the commotion of going to the doctor's office and then closing the café, they had forgotten to bring it home.

Julia stared at the bag, and then at her busy parents.

She was late — the team had probably finished their warm-up laps by now — but maybe she'd just head over to the pool and put her bathing suit back on. It was probably still wet and very cold, but Julia didn't mind. She'd probably just shiver for a few seconds, maybe a few minutes. Then she could slide into the pool and swim . . . with her *head out of the water*!

That was *such* a good idea. She needed to keep swimming. There was still a chance she wouldn't miss PBD next week — her ear would be *a lot* better by then, and Mom would see that getting her ear a little wet was no big deal.

A jolt of energy surged through Julia. She

sat up straighter and wondered why she hadn't thought of this before! Her parents wouldn't notice she was gone at all. If they did notice, all they'd have to do was look around and they'd see her in the pool, because her head would be *above* water!

A huge smile crept across Julia's face.

She moved carefully and deliberately. Quiet as a shadow, she slid off the stool.

Dad was so focused on pressing rolls that he hadn't looked in Julia's direction in ages. Mom was preoccupied talking to the center's art teacher, Stevie. Julia bent over to pick up the swim bag and slowly lifted the strap onto her shoulder.

Nobody was paying her any attention. Julia took her first step toward the part of the counter that flipped up so they could enter and exit the café. She was not even going to flip it, because sometimes it squeaked. Crouching would do just fine.

Just as she bent over, ready to duck under the counter, she heard, "Hey, Julia! What are you doing?"

Unfortunately, Stevie was facing her direction. Mom whipped around to see Julia hunched under the counter with her swim bag on her shoulder.

"Uh, hi, Stevie," Julia said awkwardly. She stood up straighter.

"Why do you have the swimming bag?" Mom asked. Then she gasped. "Julia! Were you going *swimming*?"

Julia let the bag slide off her shoulder and drop to the ground. "No!" She forcefully denied it. "I was just . . . moving the bag out of the way."

Mom put her hands on her hips. "Really?"

"Really!" Julia stood up straight and tried to sound convincing. Her cheeks started to burn.

"Uh, Julia." Stevie cleared her throat. "Your mom and I were just talking. Why don't you come sit in on my five o'clock art class?"

Stevie was the nicest teacher at the center, but still, the suggestion took her by surprise.

Julia glanced at her scowling mother. Art class wouldn't be nearly as good as swimming, like she had planned, but it was better than nothing. Better than sitting here with Mom being angry at her, that was for sure.

"Um. Okay. Thank you, that's a good idea," Julia said. She glanced at the clock on her parents' cash register. She'd have to wait forty-five minutes, but still, it was at least something to do.

The moment Stevie turned to leave, Mom whispered something into Dad's ear. Like a gopher popping out of a hole, Dad's head darted out from behind Mom's, and he glared at his daughter.

"Julia . . ." His eyes narrowed. This time, Dad actually *did* seem a little upset.

Julia looked to the ground.

Dad turned to look at his vocabulary words. Every week, he taped up a list of words in English, with their Korean equivalents, and tried to use them in everyday conversation. After he quickly scanned the list, Dad found the word he wanted.

"That was very . . . *devious* of you."

"I don't even know what that means," Julia murmured to herself.

"Were you trying to trick us?" Dad asked. Both he and Mom were staring intensely at her. They formed an angry parental wall.

Julia twisted her mouth. "Well, I wasn't trying to *trick* you. I *was* going to keep my head out of the water."

"You just need to keep your ear dry, okay?" Mom wagged a finger at Julia. For good measure, she let out an irritated huff.

"But . . ." Julia wanted to tell them about how important training for PBD was, but now did not seem to be a good time.

"Why don't you go to the library until five?" Dad suggested. He went back to slicing rolls with his big knife. "No water there," he mumbled to himself.

"Good idea!" Mom said to Dad before turning to Julia. "Don't even *think* about picking up that bag again." Her lips puckered.

Julia glanced at the bag.

"Go!" Mom pointed down the hallway. "Before I think too much about what you were trying to do and get *really* angry." Mom turned away from her and started to organize the towers of plastic containers.

Julia realized it was best to do as she was told and she headed to the library. There would definitely be no swimming today.

CHAPTER 9

Julia didn't really feel like going to the library, but it sure looked like Mom and Dad could use some time away from her. She meandered down the main hallway of the community center.

Then, suddenly, she remembered that Lorna had a new book for her! She was supposed to go to the library anyway. How silly of her to have forgotten!

Julia picked up the pace. Unlike the pool deck of the aquatic center, in the hallway, there were no strict rules about running. She shivered and ran even faster as she passed the ice rink.

The air was always chilly there. A hockey team was practicing slapshots, and the pucks hitting the sides of the rink echoed loudly.

The library was just ahead.

The sliding glass library doors were always so slow. Julia had to screech to a halt just in front of them. As soon as they slid open, she darted around, looking for Lorna.

"Miss Nam!" Lorna called from her seat behind the front desk. Julia had sprinted right past her without noticing.

As fast as she could, she circled back to the desk.

"How are you?" Lorna asked, resting on her elbows. The wrinkles in the corners of her eyes deepened.

"Ear infection. I have to take medicine." Julia frowned. "It's not disgusting, but pretty close. I'm feeling better, so I don't think I even need it anymore."

"But it's a good thing you got it checked out."

"Mom won't let me go swimming either!" Julia complained. "They're swimming right now, without *me*!" Julia leaned on Lorna's desk and laid her chin on her arms.

"It's disappointing, I know. It's only temporary, though. Your health is the most important thing."

Why did Lorna have to sound exactly like her mother?

"Sometimes those ear infections can turn really bad," Lorna said. "My daughter needed to get tubes put in."

"Tubes?" Julia suddenly felt concerned.

"Tubes to help drain the fluid from her ears. She had it done at the hospital."

"Oh," Julia said quietly. Going to the hospital to get a tube in your ear did not sound fun. She hadn't realized that fluid from an ear infection could lead to a hospital visit. Suddenly, the pink stuff didn't seem so bad after all. It was a pretty color, *and* it made her feel better. There were only nine days left of her medicine, she tried to remind herself. "Is your daughter okay?"

"Oh, it was ages ago. She's fine. Totally fine." Lorna smiled. "Now, we'd better conduct our business, don't you think? My shift is over soon."

"Yes, please!"

Lorna looked around the library in a really funny way. She liked to be silly sometimes. She almost looked like a thief who was trying not to be noticed, but her movements were so big it was impossible *not* to notice her. Lorna swiveled in her chair and leaned back, extra far. Julia was worried she'd fall over.

"Nobody's looking, right?" Lorna asked.

Julia tried not to smile. "The coast is clear."

From underneath the counter, Lorna lifted out a book and slowly handed it to Julia. "It's the latest Alleycat Adventure!" Lorna declared. "I remember you told me how much you liked the last book. This new one is called *Alleycat: Meet Raccoon.*"

Julia could not stop herself from hopping up and down a few times. This was the best thing that had happened in two days! She loved this series. That Alleycat got into so much trouble all the time. When the third book had come out, Julia had to put it on hold. She started off as number twenty-four on the waitlist. It took forever to finally get a copy.

"Thank you, Lorna! I'll ask Mom to give you the biggest piece of tofu in the pot next time!"

Lorna smiled. "I *do* like tofu. Now, don't forget our deal — you bring it back tomorrow, so I can put it in general circulation. Got it?"

"I will read it tonight!" Julia promised.

"That's my little reader. Sorry, I've got to go now. But I'll see you tomorrow." Lorna twisted her dark brown hair with its streaks of silver into a messy bun.

"Lorna, before I go . . ." Julia hesitated.

Librarians had the answers to all sorts of questions — Julia had one question she needed to ask. Sometimes it's good to get lots of different opinions. Dr. Deol seemed smart, but maybe she didn't know *everything*. She had even admitted that she wasn't too experienced with earplugs. Julia's mother knew lots of stuff too, but she wasn't exactly an ear infection expert.

Lorna, on the other hand, was an information expert — there was even a sign in front of her desk that said "Information Desk." If you sat behind a desk with that sign, it meant you had answers.

"Do you know how I can stop water from getting in my ear, like, *right now*?" Julia asked self-consciously.

"Simple! Don't go near water!" Lorna laughed.

That was not the answer Julia had been hoping for. "Don't be silly."

"I'm not, sweetie. If your mother doesn't want you swimming just for a little bit, well, it's simple." Lorna paused to make sure Julia was listening. "Just wait."

Just wait! Julia was going to miss four practices *and* PBD! Lorna clearly did not love to swim. Julia thought about asking Lorna how she'd feel going without coffee for ten days, but actually, Julia had never seen her holding a coffee cup. Instead, she asked her, "What if you had to go ten days without . . . *tofu?*"

Lorna looked surprised and a tiny bit anxious. "No tofu? Well, that would be hard, wouldn't it? But I'm a big girl. I could eat something else."

That was another answer Julia was not expecting or hoping for. *I'm a big girl, too!* Julia thought. "But you'd miss it, right?"

"Of course! But in the meantime, I might try other yummy things."

"But you wouldn't *choose* not to eat tofu, would you?" Julia thought that was a good comeback.

"No, I would never *choose* to give up something I love! *But* sometimes when what you love to eat most isn't available, you are forced to choose something else. When you choose something else, you might be in a for a nice surprise!"

"Well . . . ," Julia said as she rubbed her toe into the carpet, "Stevie said I could come to her art class today. I guess that's like eating something else."

"That's the spirit," Lorna said. She leaned back in her chair. Then her telephone rang. She reached for it as she said, "See you later, Miss Nam."

Julia nodded and, with her new book tucked under her arm, she turned to leave.

Julia liked Stevie and her art class, but she knew that, no matter what, nothing was more delicious to her than swimming.

CHAPTER 10

After stowing her new Alleycat book safely back at the sushi café, Julia headed to Stevie's art room. It was almost five. She knew exactly where to go — second floor, down at the end of the hallway.

When she arrived, Julia stood frozen in the open doorway. Nobody had mentioned that the art class was for five- and six-year-olds. Julia was taller than everybody — by a lot! On her swim team, she always felt so little, but here, it was the opposite.

"Julia!" Stevie said breathlessly. She was

helping a girl put on an art smock. "Come in!"

It was hard to mistake Stevie for anything other than an art teacher. The paint-splattered clothes made it pretty obvious. She also had unique eyeglasses. The frames were bright red to match the red streak in her otherwise blond hair.

"Ow! My head's stuck!" the girl Stevie was helping complained.

Stevie yanked the art smock down and said, "There!"

Everything Stevie said seemed to end with an exclamation mark, like she was always really excited.

"Where should I sit?" Julia asked.

"I set up a table just for you!" Stevie pointed to the corner.

"Thank you."

"You can make anything you like. Just head to the supply cabinet and pick out what you need!" Then Stevie was gone, chasing after one of her students who had escaped before putting his smock on.

Sometimes little kids were not good at listening to instructions.

Julia stood in front of the cabinet, which was bursting with different supplies: small tubs of paint, boxes full of pastels, bins full of glue sticks, and bags full of pom-poms. She rummaged around before she accidentally tipped over a brown bottle. The lid of the bottle came off and a thick fluid started to slowly dribble out.

Julia quickly snatched the bottle and placed it upright. She glanced over at Stevie, who was trying very hard to get the attention of her students. She was not very successful. Her face was turning pink with the effort.

Deciding not to bother Stevie, Julia used her hand to sweep up the mess, which was white and very gooey. It seemed like glue, but it was much thicker than the kind she used at school.

Julia did her best to clean up. Luckily, the spill was only about the size of one slice of

California roll. She walked over to the sink to wash her hands. Another girl was already there, rinsing a sponge very thoroughly.

While she waited, Julia looked at her hand. The glue had gone between her fingers, and when she pulled her fingers apart, they stuck together for a brief moment.

Interesting, she thought.

~~~~~~~~~

The day had seemed extra long without swimming. After the art class, Julia wandered the hallways of the community center. She didn't want to go straight back to the café because she'd be too close to the pool. Saleema didn't even come at closing time today. It was somebody Julia had never seen before who came to do the pickup for Shared Meals. By the time they had finally got home, she was ready to go to bed.

Lying under the covers, Julia noticed a bit of blue pastel stuck under her fingernail from Stevie's class. The pastel was waxy, thick, and just a tiny bit gummy. As she picked at the sticky stuff that wasn't supposed to be under her nail, she couldn't help but think about the extra water in her ear that wasn't supposed to be there either.

She closed her eyes and shook her head quickly, side to side, hoping to hear it sloshing around. But she didn't hear anything. She wondered if that meant all the fluid Dr. Deol had seen was gone now.

A few minutes after she had curled up with her blanket tight around her, Julia noticed that she was feeling a tiny bit hot. She sat up, lifted her blanket to get some air under it, and repositioned herself with her arms over the covers. She felt more comfortable now.

She wondered if her parents were just being *too* careful. After all, she couldn't *hear* any water in her ear, and she was feeling better already! No pain at all! Being careful was good, but sometimes being careful was no fun. She hugged her huge stuffed whale, Korae, before tucking him into her elbow.

Her mother knocked gently on the door. "Are you feeling okay?"

"I'm feeling great!" Julia thought dropping a hint about how good she was feeling might be helpful. "Super great! It's like my ear is totally normal! I'm pretty sure that the water or fluid or whatever Dr. Deol saw is all gone!"

Mom suppressed a smile. "Oh, I see." She sat on the edge of Julia's bed. Her mother didn't seem upset anymore, and Julia was glad.

"I don't see what the big deal is. Dr. Deol said swimming was probably okay! I promise, I pinky swear, I won't dive deep. I just want to swim." She sat up and stuck out her right pinky and waited for her mother to do the same.

Instead, her mother clicked her tongue. Julia dropped her hand.

"I know you think you are like Korae."
Mom patted the whale. When she said the word,
it sounded like *Go-reh*. Julia couldn't say the
word the way Mom did. "But sometimes you
have to remember you are a little girl, not a sea
animal." Her mother tapped the end of Julia's
nose with her finger. "Your health is important.
I read that sometimes ear infections need
treatment at the hospital."

Julia sighed. This was just like what
Lorna had said about her daughter. Julia

threw herself back down on her pillow. "Okay, Eomma, okay. Good night."

"Good night." Mom closed the door.

Finally, it was time for Julia to read her book from the library.

She looked at the details of the book's front cover. Alleycat's fur was a mess, and Raccoon looked so funny. She smiled just looking at the picture. This book was going to be hilarious.

Alleycat and his new enemy Raccoon were fighting over recycling. Alleycat liked to fight with everyone. She was so silly! It was even funnier when a plastic container landed on Raccoon's head like a hat.

Julia quietly chuckled before she continued to read each panel. She liked to linger over every drawing. If she looked at the pictures too quickly, she missed some details.

At first, Raccoon thought that the plastic container was irritating. He was going to remove it. But Raccoon soon learned that the plastic container had one good use. It protected him from the bird droppings from the messy pigeon family who lived on the wire above the alley.

Julia suddenly put the book down and stopped reading. If a plastic container could protect Raccoon from bird droppings, she wondered if it could do something else — protect her ear from water! The plastic container was poop-proof and . . . *waterproof.* Ideas tumbled around in her head.

Julia stayed up reading later than usual. She didn't want to break Lorna's deal, so she needed to finish the book and return it tomorrow.

While she read, one idea in particular grew and grew in her head. Sushi on the Go! had lots of plastic containers around. Stacks taller than her. If they could hold miso soup *in,* couldn't they also hold water *out*?

Just before turning off her light, she snuggled Korae tight and whispered into its ear, "Do you think it would work for me?"

Korae bobbed its head up and down.

There was just one detail that troubled her. How could she stick a plastic container on the side of her head over her ear? Raccoon's container fit over his small head nicely. But there wasn't a container big enough at the café to fit her whole head into. There *had* to be a way to attach it, though.

When she finally fell asleep, she dreamed only about sticky things.

CHAPTER 11

During school on Friday, Julia couldn't think of anything else but PBD. It was just six days away, after all. She couldn't even enjoy Pizza Friday at lunch, the only day she didn't pack sushi to eat.

After school, Julia sat on her stool and stared through the glass wall. She realized that even though it wasn't as bad as watching the team swim without her like yesterday, she didn't like watching the swimmers at the public swim splash around either.

As a way of keeping her eyes off the pool, she worked hard on her *Marine Animals Intense*

Dot-to-Dot book. This book required a very sharp pencil, a magnifying glass, and a headlamp, because the numbers were so small and the lighting in the community center wasn't bright enough for detailed work.

There was something wonderful about watching a jumble of random dots turn into a whole picture.

Deeply focused, Julia didn't notice Olivia Huang standing just a few feet away from her until Olivia spoke.

"Why weren't you at practice yesterday?"

Julia jumped. Her headlamp slipped down her forehead slightly. She pulled it off and closed her book. Without her hair wet and in her regular clothes, Julia hardly recognized her. Olivia had her hair clipped on the side with a pretty red pin, and she wore a fleece jacket and jeans.

"I saw you here and I wondered," Olivia continued.

For some reason, Julia didn't want to tell Olivia anything. She tried changing the subject

instead. "What are *you* doing here today, anyway?"

"I have my Les Petits Amis class today."

Julia knew the teacher of that French program. Hubert. When you saw his name spelled, it looked nothing like how it was pronounced. He pronounced it *Hu-bear*. Maybe French words were just as confusing to learn as English words. *Hu-bear* sometimes bought something to eat from the Nams.

Usually a spicy salmon roll. Julia knew everybody's favorites.

"So, why weren't you at swim club?" Olivia persisted. "Are you not feeling well or something?"

It was better when Olivia was wearing her dark goggles and Julia couldn't look into her brown eyes. Her eyes were piercing and insistent — and also *nosy*.

"I'm not supposed to swim, that's all," Julia said, hoping a vague answer would send Olivia away.

"Why not? Are you quitting?" Olivia continued to grill Julia.

"No!" Julia was horrified that Olivia would even *think* such a thing. "I just can't swim *right now*. But I'll be back!"

"What's with all the secrecy? Geez . . ."

Olivia seemed like the type that couldn't take a hint, so Julia decided to tell her. Maybe Olivia's curiosity would be satisfied and she'd just leave already. "I have an ear infection, okay? There, I told you. Happy now?" Julia snapped.

"Can't you just wear one of those earplugs?"

What a know-it-all. As if they hadn't already considered that. Why wouldn't Olivia just *go away*?

Julia sighed and glanced at her overly careful mother. "It's not that kind of infection. Those earplugs probably wouldn't work. Anyway, my mom thinks it's best if I just take my gross pink medicine and stay out of the water for now."

"Better to be safe!" Mom called out from behind the cash register before she went back to helping a customer.

"Oh, I see." Finally, it looked as if Olivia was satisfied after her interrogation.

Julia opened her dot-to-dot book again.

"That's too bad, because you're going to miss PBD," Olivia said.

"I know." Julia was starting to feel very annoyed.

Olivia leaned in over the counter. "Yeah, but what you *don't* know is that this year, our age bracket can go to the regional meet if your personal best is fast enough." A dimple formed in Olivia's right cheek, as though she was trying to hold back a smile. "But I guess you can't improve on your PB if you can't swim."

"Regional meet? What? I thought we were too young!" Julia was shocked. She had missed *one* practice and some *huge* news.

"Not this year. Coach said it's a new rule or something. Swimmers as young as nine can go if your qualifying time is fast enough. See you around."

I'm nine! Julia said to herself. Dazed, Julia kept her eyes fixed on Olivia's back as she walked away. Her book slipped out of her hands and landed on the floor.

The regional meet. It was where all the best local swimmers raced. That was where Julia belonged. But she wouldn't be able to qualify.

CHAPTER 12

"How do you feel this morning?" Dad asked Julia. He was sitting on the sofa watching a Korean drama on his tablet.

"Fine," she answered automatically. But she knew why Dad was asking. As soon as she spoke, though, she realized it was the truth. Her ear didn't bother her at all!

"Good news! Still, it's time for your morning dose."

Julia sighed and mentally counted the days. She had seen the doctor Wednesday, had missed practice Thursday, and Olivia had told her the upsetting news on Friday.

Today was Monday. She bent her fingers down one by one. That meant she still needed to take the medicine for another *five* days. And that meant she was going to miss three more practices, including the PBD, which was now an even bigger deal than ever.

Her mind had been preoccupied with this dilemma all weekend. Could she still swim on Personal Best Day? Somehow? The small idea that had started in Stevie's art class had become a big, unshakable idea after reading Alleycat's latest book, and it still stuck with her.

She tried not to think about it right now. First, she had to take her medicine.

"Appa. My medicine?" Julia asked, wanting to get it over with.

"Sorry!" Dad walked to the kitchen while staring at the screen. "It's the newest episode of my favorite drama. Almost done." After a few seconds, Dad finally put down his device.

Then he started to measure out the bad-tasting chalky pink liquid in the special measuring spoon that the pharmacy had given them. He looked around the kitchen before he whispered, "I'll give you a few of these after, okay?" He held his finger up to his lips before opening a cabinet that was too high for Julia to reach. He pulled down a small bag and showed her.

Jelly beans!

"How many do I get?" Julia asked.

"Shh!" Dad looked over his shoulder.

"Are you bargaining?" He
seemed surprised.

"How many?" Julia
repeated. She stood firm.

"Four," Dad whispered.
"Hurry, before Eomma comes."

"One of each color."
Julia didn't know how many
that was, but it was probably
more than four.

"Ah, expert haggler."
Dad gave up and patted the
top of her head. "Okay, take
this first." He held out the
spoonful of medicine.

Julia leaned closer to her
father and gulped it down. She
grimaced and shook her shoulders.

"Quick!" She stuck out her hand and
shook it impatiently, waiting for the jelly beans.

Her father ripped open the bag and
fished around.

"Wow, this pack has so many different kinds!" He placed one in Julia's hand. She popped it into her mouth while she waited for more.

"What's going on?" Mom walked into the kitchen.

Dad jumped and nearly dropped the bag.

Julia gulped the last remains of the candy in her mouth and closed her hand tightly over the ones she hadn't eaten yet.

"Jelly beans! It's only eight in the morning!" Mom strode next to Dad and snatched the bag out of his hands.

He shrugged his shoulders. "She took her medicine! *You* give her the evening dose."

"I'm going to want chocolate then," Julia told her mother. She smashed all the remaining jelly beans into her mouth.

Mom laughed quietly and put her arm around Julia. "Come on, time to go."

Just before heading off to school, Julia remembered something. The jelly beans had distracted her. Before leaving, she needed to take a look in the junk drawer in the kitchen. The idea that kept sploshing and splashing in her head all weekend needed some supplies.

The drawer was full of old elastic bands from newspapers, pads of paper that seemed to always come free in the mail, pens that sometimes worked, and other assorted items that her parents never wanted to throw away.

This drawer also contained tape (two different kinds) and glue (three different kinds). This drawer was extremely useful.

She wasn't sure which of these items would work best, but Julia thought it was important to be prepared for everything. She knew she was going to need sticky things. The stickier the better. There may have been five days of medicine left, but she had only *three* days before PBD, and she had to do something about it.

At school, the sticky stuff in her backpack was on her mind all day. Julia couldn't concentrate. Maricel noticed too.

"Is something the matter?" she asked. "Are you still sad about missing swimming?"

Julia couldn't fool Maricel. Maricel knew everything about her: when she was mad, when she was happy, when she was sad. Maricel was the best kind of friend.

Julia nodded. "I'll never not be sad about missing swimming."

"If a human being and a fish could be mashed into one person, I think that would be you," Maricel said.

"*Bloop, bloop, bloop.*" Julia puffed out her cheeks and did her best impersonation of a fish blowing air bubbles.

Maricel laughed. Her black wavy hair bounced around her shoulders, and the warm, brown skin of her round cheeks flushed. That was Maricel's thing — the longest and loudest laugh in the class. You could hear her from all the way down the other end of the hallway.

Ms. Mendez looked up from her desk and peered over the top of her glasses. "Maricel . . ." she warned.

Maricel did her best to calm down and work on her math problems. "No, seriously, are you okay?" Maricel whispered once she had recovered.

"Do you . . ." Julia hesitated.

Maricel put her pencil down to listen.

"Do you know anything about . . . glues and tapes?" Julia asked.

"Huh?" Maricel looked confused.

"Like, the best ones."

Maricel gazed out the window as she pondered Julia's question. "Well, you could experiment. Trial and error? Remember when we did that for science? Like which design makes the best paper airplane?"

Julia nodded. Trial and error. That sounded good. She should test out the sticky stuff.

Maricel continued, "Or you could ask the really nice librarian at the community center. She'd probably know."

"Those are both good ideas."

Being an information expert, Lorna was sure to know something about sticky stuff. Lorna hadn't really helped with her question the other day about how to stop water from getting in her ear, but today's question was going to be completely different. Maybe today's answer would solve all her problems.

CHAPTER 13

Once she got to the community center in the afternoon, Julia dashed to the library to see Lorna.

After running through the sliding glass doors, Julia skidded to a halt. Lorna was sitting at a computer and was busy helping . . . Olivia! Julia was surprised to see Olivia at the community center on a non-training day, *again*! Julia walked cautiously toward them. Olivia glanced over at Julia but didn't say anything — she just kept talking to Lorna.

Julia sighed. It was very frustrating

because there was the *big* idea, an *important* idea, that had been niggling at her all day — all weekend, in fact! But now, it looked like she would have to wait to get some answers. She'd already waited throughout the school day. She'd waited during the car ride to the community center, and now she had to wait some more.

Olivia was clearly hogging Lorna's time. Olivia kept pointing to the screen and asking so many questions. Whatever Lorna's answer was, it never seemed to be enough for Olivia.

Standing at the side of the computer station, Julia tapped her foot impatiently and bobbed her head around so Lorna couldn't ignore her. It felt like the big idea was going to burst in her brain.

Lorna raised a finger to show that she knew Julia was waiting, but that did not make Olivia go any faster.

Julia paced behind them. She put her fist up to her mouth to try to calm her racing heart.

The question she wanted to ask Lorna was
burning inside her.

    Still Olivia talked.

    Julia paced some more. Then she tried
swaying her head from side to side so she was
hard to miss.

    Olivia eyed Julia but continued to ask
questions.

    The feeling that Olivia was talking a lot

on purpose overcame Julia. She couldn't stop herself and said, "Lorna! I can't wait anymore!" Julia tugged at Lorna's sleeve.

Lorna said to Olivia, "I'm sorry. Could you wait one second?"

Olivia nodded and flipped through a book.

Lorna motioned for Julia to take a few steps away from the computers. Lorna scanned the bookshelf next to them. "Ah, look, Dewey decimal call number 395. The perfect place to stop. You see, this section has books on *manners*." Lorna crossed her arms over her woolly sweater.

Julia looked to the ground.

"Now, Julia," Lorna said, softening her tone. "You know I like you and your family very much, but this is no way to behave. I was helping another person. My job in this library is to help *everybody*."

Julia frowned and she felt her face turn warm. "But Olivia has too many questions!"

Olivia looked up from her book and

glared at Julia. "Questions are the sign of a curious mind!"

A nosy curious mind, Julia thought. She opened her mouth to say something to Olivia, but a familiar voice startled her.

"Julia! There you are!" The voice was a little loud for the library, and everybody turned to look. It was Coach Marissa.

"Coach?" Julia was surprised to see her in the library.

"Your parents said you'd be here," Coach said, slightly out of breath. "Listen, I'm in a rush, but I wanted to make sure you're still in the loop. I'm sorry, I should have done this sooner."

Julia forgot about Olivia and Lorna and focused on Coach Marissa.

"You know you're going to miss PBD, right? Your mom told me about . . ." Coach pointed to her ear to show Julia she knew what was going on.

Julia nodded.

"I know you're probably upset. Slightly worse news is that your age bracket can go to regionals this year too — with a qualifying time that I have to submit by the end of next week."

It was too hard to talk, so Julia swallowed hard and just kept nodding. Lorna put her hand on Julia's shoulder.

"But I was thinking, you know you are still part of the team, right? I wanted to think of a way for you to participate. Do you want to come to the junior practice Thursday and be my official team timer?"

The thought of timing her teammates somehow made Julia feel even worse. Julia shook her head no.

"Ah, okay," Coach said. "I understand. It will be hard for you."

Julia felt like she must be the unluckiest girl in the entire community center. This ear infection had come at the worst time!

Olivia stepped away from the computer

and said to Lorna, "I think I have enough information, thank you." She turned quickly on her heel and left. Julia was sure that Olivia had smirked in her direction. Julia's cheeks burned.

"But you *are* the youngest on the team. There's always next season. There will be another big meet then." Coach smiled, but Julia could not return it. "I've got to get back to the senior team." She quickly waved goodbye. "Come Thursday and help, if you want."

Next *season*? That was just another word for next *year*.

"That might be fun," Lorna said as they watched Coach leave. "Helping to keep track of the times."

"But it will be other people's times," Julia said unhappily. "Not mine."

Julia knew she had to get back in the pool, and fast. She would not wait for next season's PBD.

CHAPTER 14

After Coach left, Julia felt like she had been run over by a big truck.

"Oh, this is disappointing news, for sure," Lorna said. "But you could still go out and support your teammates, couldn't you?"

"But PBD means *Personal* Best Day, not *Team* Best Day," Julia replied. Wearily, she leaned against a bookshelf. All of her energy had drained away.

"Why not turn that *P* into a *T*?" Lorna chuckled. "*T*BD!"

Julia thought that joke sounded a lot like

something Dad would say. She didn't even laugh one tiny bit. She couldn't.

"You're part of the Vipers, aren't you?" Lorna asked.

Julia nodded.

"You'll still be part of the Vipers even if you can't swim on PBD."

"I know." Julia looked at the ground. She knew Lorna was just trying to say nice things to make her feel better. But Julia didn't feel better at all. The only thing that *could* make her feel better was getting an official PBD time!

"Now, before Coach found you, you wanted to talk to me about something?"

Julia had almost completely forgotten! Without Olivia around, she could finally tell Lorna the *real* reason she needed to talk to her. Julia had thought her big question was important before, but now, it felt more urgent than ever. There was no time to waste!

"I just need to know what the best sticky stuff is! Is there a book or a website that can help me?" Julia already had a wide assortment of sticky stuff in her backpack, but, just like Maricel had suggested, she wanted Lorna's professional opinion on her vague idea too. "That's all I need to know."

"The best sticky stuff?" Lorna asked.

"I want to . . ." Julia paused. "I have something I want to stick to another something."

The confused look on Lorna's face suddenly made Julia feel strange about her question.

"I don't know off the top of my head, but I guess we could do a little research. Do you want to give me more specifics? What are you trying to do? Exactly?" Lorna asked.

"I want to . . . stick something together." Julia looked at Lorna's face carefully.

Lorna chuckled. "Yes, that part I understand. What I don't understand is *what* you want to stick together or why." Then she started to look suspicious. "What have you got planned?" A big wrinkle started to form right where her nose and eyes met.

Suddenly, Julia decided she didn't want to ask Lorna to help her find information about sticky stuff. Not if she had to tell Lorna *exactly* what she was thinking. Maybe Lorna wouldn't approve. After all, Lorna had agreed with her mother that it was best to wait before swimming again. Lorna didn't seem to realize how important getting back in the pool really was.

Julia's heart started to thump loudly in her chest. This was not going as she had hoped. "Never mind! It's nothing. I have to go see my parents now."

Julia scampered out of the library without looking back. She had hoped that an information expert could help, and now Julia wasn't so sure. But all was not lost. She still had one more plan — experiment by trial and error.

Julia returned to Sushi on the Go! with only the same vague idea she had already been turning over in her mind.

Her parents were very busy and did not pay her much attention. There was a line of customers.

Through the glass wall, Julia watched the senior team warm up on the deck. Then she saw them dive, one by one, into their lanes and take off. The water started to churn. Some of them warmed up with front crawl, but some started with the breaststroke.

She watched Coach Marissa wheel a whiteboard close to the water. Then Coach dragged a large, wheeled bin full of equipment next to the pool's edge and began placing the electronic timing pads in each lane. Each of these pads was connected to a display board that showed times with red LED numbers. The senior team was doing their PBD — *today*!

When Coach was finished, she went back to the whiteboard and turned it. Julia could see it better now. If she squinted, she could read what it said.

The board was covered with a grid

containing the names of swimmers, their best event, and their previous best time. In the last column was an empty spot, for their time today. Everybody was going to want to replace their old time with a new, better time. Julia's heart fluttered at the thought of the senior team pouring all they had into their swims.

After the warm-up, the swimmers gathered on deck and listened to Coach give some instructions. Although she couldn't hear what Coach was saying, Julia knew it was a kind of pep talk. The swimmers nodded their heads and took their positions to do more training laps.

Julia watched the senior team leaping into the water with determined focus. Even though the official timing hadn't even started yet, they seemed single-minded. They all wanted their PB swim today.

Their focus made Julia feel even more resolved. She was *not* going to miss *her* chance to swim on PBD Thursday. She still had hope.

Her parents were still helping customers, so she snuck behind them and reached for an empty plastic soup container. She quickly placed it over her right ear. It was the perfect size!

She picked up her backpack and placed the plastic bowl inside. She needed to know if her idea would work. There was no better time to find out than right now.

"I'm going to the washroom!" she announced to her parents.

"Hmm," they said to her without really looking. Her father was in the middle of slicing. Her mother was at the cash register.

Julia marched down the main hallway of the community center, in her backpack an

 empty soup container and various sticky things.

CHAPTER 15

The washrooms at the community center were often busy. With so many people coming and going every day, it sure kept the staff, like Ms. Fargas, busy.

But there was one secret washroom — the staff washroom. Unless you knew the special code, it was locked. And Julia knew the special code.

She pressed the 3 and the 6 at the same time, then pressed the 1 and the 4 at the same time. The red light flashed, and the door stayed locked. It was hard to do it right on the first try.

They made it tricky on purpose.

Julia set her mind to doing it again but making sure she did it properly this time.

Once the green light flashed on the keypad, she was in.

The washroom was a single large space. She flicked the latch on the door to read "Occupied" so nobody would bother her.

Julia plunked her backpack down on the floor and rummaged through it. She took out a roll of clear tape, the kind you use to wrap presents, and then a roll of masking tape. The kind of tape you used when you couldn't find any other tape.

Next, she pulled out a bottle of white glue, the kind you use for arts and crafts projects. Then a glue stick. And finally, a small tube of something called Rhinoceros Glue. Julia read the label. It said, "For extra-tough stubborn jobs!"

Julia considered her choices. She had experience with four of the five sticky things.

She picked at the roll of masking tape with her fingernail until she was able to pull a layer of it away from the rest of the roll. When the length of tape was as long as a pencil, Julia ripped it off with her teeth. She felt it between her fingers to test the stickiness. This tape was the un-stickiest tape ever made! She crumpled it into a ball and threw it in the trash.

She needed something better. Something stronger. She needed to use the glue that was made for tough jobs. It said so, right on the label.

She swept her hair away from her ear and pinned it back with a bobby pin. Next, she unscrewed the cap of the Rhinoceros Glue and dabbed it gently around the rim of the plastic soup container. To make sure she placed it correctly, she looked at herself in the bathroom mirror.

The instructions said, "For the best results, hold the bond in place for 30 seconds."

Julia looked carefully at the thin beads of glue she had just squeezed onto the rim of the

bowl. She took a deep breath. Then Julia pressed the soup container over her right ear and counted to thirty.

Thirty seconds seemed like such a long time, but Julia made sure to follow the instructions exactly.

When she let go, the soup container stayed in place. Her heart leapt with joy. She looked back at her reflection in the mirror and was thrilled her idea had worked.

Now she would be able to go swimming tomorrow, she was sure of that! The soup container would keep water out of her ear the same way it kept soup inside!

Julia did a little happy dance. She tapped the plastic bowl. It made a loud *thump, thump* in her ear. The noise was loud, and she could hear it perfectly. Her ear was getting better and better!

She sighed, feeling very satisfied. Then she remembered she should probably get back to her parents. This test run had gone perfectly. There was no need to keep experimenting.

Julia had found an answer. She would convince her parents that she could go swimming on Thursday, and she'd get her best time for the regional meet. What could her mother say against this idea? The bowl was *waterproof.*

Now, she needed to take the bowl off. Standing in front of the mirror, Julia pulled at it. Part of it came away quickly, but one part didn't want to. The part just under her ear near her jaw felt stuck to her skin. It hurt when she tugged it.

Julia started to panic. She realized suddenly that sticky stuff might stay sticky for longer than she wanted. She read the instructions on the tube again.

This time, she read the *whole* label.

CAUTION: Avoid touching skin with glue. It will be extremely difficult to remove.

Now her heart sank with despair. Why

hadn't she read the whole label *before?* She dropped the Rhinoceros Glue in the sink and stared at her reflection.

She pulled at the bowl again.

"Ouch!" she yelped. "Come off!" She felt annoyed at the bowl and at herself.

But the bowl would not come off.

The Rhinoceros Glue was indeed the stickiest stuff in the world.

The idea of walking around the community center with a plastic bowl stuck to the side of her head left Julia feeling humiliated.

She wished she had a big jacket with a giant hood. Sometimes the older kids at the community center walked around with their hoods over their heads, and that looked cool. But Julia didn't have a hood. All she had was her jean jacket.

She slipped it off and put the jacket on top of her head like a hooded cape. Checking

herself in the mirror one more time, she felt confident that nobody would notice the bowl.

Carefully, leaving no trace of her time in the washroom, Julia packed up all her tape and glue and headed back to her parents.

As she walked quickly down the main hall of the community center, she passed several people, but nobody stopped and stared at her.

Not one person seemed to notice a small girl with a jean jacket on her head and a plastic bowl covering her ear. This small bit of good news buoyed Julia's spirits a tiny bit. Maybe her parents wouldn't notice either! They were probably very busy with lots of customers.

Julia made her way past the ice rink, and the closer she got to Sushi on the Go! the harder it was to move one foot in front of the other.

As she came closer to her family's café, she realized, unfortunately, that her parents had no customers to distract them — not a single one! Mom glanced over at her approaching daughter and then quickly went back to slicing green onions before doing a double take.

"Julia?" Mom put down her knife.

Trying her best to pretend everything was fine, Julia walked behind the counter. She dropped her backpack on the floor and sat on her stool in the corner. *Just act natural,* she told herself.

Dad stopped organizing the take-out containers and looked at Julia.

"Are you cold?" he asked her.

Her eyes popped open. "Yes!" she said, a little too loudly.

Her mother took a few steps closer, and Julia shrank back into her seat. "Do you want some soup?" Mom asked.

The thought of having soup from a container, like the one stuck to her head, did not sound especially good to her at that moment. In fact, the idea left her feeling a bit queasy, but Julia nodded anyway.

Her mother eyed her with a look of concern. Julia found it difficult to look back at her.

After pouring one ladleful of soup, Mom put down the plastic bowl and said, "Tell me. What's wrong?"

Julia did not know how her mother could tell. She thought she was doing a very excellent job of pretending everything was fine.

After several seconds of biting her bottom lip, Julia realized she could not wear her jean jacket hooded cape all day, even if she wanted to. Her head was starting to feel very hot.

"I have a problem," Julia finally confessed.

The phone rang and her mother held up a finger, telling Julia to wait.

Just when she was ready to admit what was going on, she had to wait, *again*. She looked up to the ceiling and tried to find some patience.

It was a take-out order, and while her mother scribbled down notes on a pad of paper, Julia sat and waited.

This seemed to be an extra-long order. Julia sat on her hands. The customer on the phone kept talking! Julia breathed slowly in and out, because finding patience was sometimes very challenging.

Finally, her mother passed the slip of paper to her father.

"Okay, tell me," Mom said as she crouched down and looked Julia in the eye.

When her mother crouched like that, Julia knew her mother was really listening.

Julia felt her lips turn into a frown. She didn't want to show Mom. But she had a bowl stuck to the side of her head! How could she *not* show her? Her bottom lip started to quiver.

"Eomma, I'm sorry!"

Julia slipped her jean jacket off her head. Her hair flew around in a staticky mess, but it couldn't hide the bowl stuck to the side of her head.

Mom raised her hand to her mouth and gasped.

CHAPTER 16

"What happened?" Mom tried to pull the bowl away from Julia's ear. "How can this be?" She couldn't make sense of what she was seeing.

"Ouch! It's stuck to my skin!"

Dad rushed over, wiping his hands on his apron.

Julia, ever hopeful, asked, "You know how to get this off, right, Appa?"

Dad tilted his head, unsure. "What did you use?"

"Rhinoceros Glue."

Dad looked stunned. "We used that to glue the broken tile in the kitchen!"

Julia's mother started muttering in Korean. When she did that, Julia knew she was in trouble.

"Why did you do this?" Mom begged, looking closer at the spot under Julia's ear near her jaw where the container was firmly fixed. The glue was also stuck to large sections of Julia's hair above her ear.

"I *really* wanted to keep swimming," Julia confessed, looking down at the ground.

Dad frowned. "It was only five more days."

There it was again: another adult talking about how it was *only* a few days without swimming. There may have been only five more, but what about the five she'd already missed?

"Appa, can you go *ten days* without watching your favorite Korean dramas?" Julia asked. She tried not to sound angry, even though she was upset.

He pressed his lips together and looked away.

For just a moment, she had been puffed up with indignation, but now, her outrage faded. "It's hard to stop doing the thing you love, right?" Julia hoped her father would understand.

Dad's eyes wrinkled in the corners. "I have Korean drama problem."

"It's not a problem!" Julia exclaimed. "You just really like it, a lot."

"Too much, maybe," Mom teased as she smiled at Dad.

"Also, this part is really important." Julia made sure her parents were listening. "It's PBD on Thursday." Julia paused. Then she added, "*Plus* there's the regional swim meet. They changed the rules! I could compete this year! But I can't go unless I get timed during PBD and have an official qualifying time!"

The hard look on her parents' faces softened slightly. Julia felt a little relieved.

Maybe they were finally starting to understand.

"I really, really want to go to the regional swim meet."

"Everything okay?" a voice from the other side of the counter asked loudly.

Lorna craned her neck around to see what was going on. Mom and Dad stepped aside just enough for her to get a glimpse of Julia sitting on the stool.

"Julia," she breathed. Her hand went up to her mouth.

"Do you know how to remove Rhinoceros Glue?" Dad asked Lorna.

"For extra-tough stubborn jobs?" Lorna repeated the words from the label. "I don't know right now, but let's look it up." Lorna pulled her cellphone out of her back pocket.

"Librarians know everything, right?" Julia said hopefully.

"Librarians know lots of stuff," Lorna agreed. "And what we don't know, we know how to find the answer." She winked.

"Come, sit." Mom ushered Lorna behind the counter and gave her a stool to sit on. She immediately started to ladle soup into a container for Lorna. "Make her a roll," Mom told Dad.

He nodded and washed his hands. "I know what Lorna likes."

"Thank you." Lorna took the bowl of soup and slurped it from the rim. She didn't even take her eyes off the screen. "Okay!" she announced. "There are a few possibilities!"

"Oh, thank you!" Mom said gratefully.

"Don't thank me yet. We need supplies. Soap. You have soap? Of course you have soap!"

"Should I close down the café?" Dad asked. A few people had started to gather. Julia was not sure if they were ordering or watching.

"No, no. I've got this," Lorna said. "Your wife can help. You keep feeding the hungry customers."

"I think they're only hungry to find out what happens to me." Julia brooded, while she

felt her cheeks grow hotter and hotter. Instead of just a few people watching, now there was a large crowd gathered around.

One of the usual customers, who worked in the gym, was just standing there eating sushi out of a container with his fingers, waiting to see what happened next.

"I need a bucket, a cloth, and some soap," Lorna declared. "Oh, wait. You probably can't get your ear too wet, can you?" she asked Julia.

Julia shook her head. "That's why I was gluing the bowl to my head in the first place!" Her shoulders slumped.

"Scratch that!" Lorna looked at her phone again. "Acetone! Where can I get acetone?"

"Acetone? I've got some in the maintenance closet." Ms. Fargas poked her head through the crowd.

"Hi, Ms. Fargas! That's great!" Lorna said. "Off you go. Be quick!"

Ms. Fargas left her cart of cleaning supplies right where it was and scurried away.

"I wish we had cotton balls," Lorna said to herself.

"I've got some in the art room!" Stevie volunteered. Julia hadn't even noticed Stevie standing there in the crowd.

"Well, what are you waiting for?" Lorna asked.

Stevie scratched the tip of her nose, which had a streak of yellow paint across it, and said, "I'll be right back!" But then she quickly turned around and said, "Mr. Nam! I actually did come to order. Can you make me two avocado and cucumber rolls?"

"Got it!" Dad said.

Julia looked at the faces in the crowd. She didn't know everybody, but she knew a lot of people — too many. She wished she were invisible. She would have settled for a fabric privacy curtain that she could have whipped around herself. It felt like the entire community center was watching her.

"While we wait, we should soak the skin

in warm water as best we can." Lorna looked puzzled. "Awkward spot."

Mom nodded in agreement. Julia also nodded in agreement. This whole thing was awkward.

Julia's face started to burn even hotter than before.

"A wet towel?" Mom suggested.

"Sure." Lorna shrugged.

Julia watched her mother grab a towel from the counter. She ran it through warm water until it was soaking wet. After a light squeeze, she brought it over to Julia. It dripped a few times on the floor.

"Let me do it," Julia insisted. Julia held the towel against the edge of bowl where it met her skin and hair. She had never felt so ridiculous in her life. She wondered if her mother had an extra towel to cover her face.

Just when Julia thought things couldn't get worse, she locked eyes with Olivia.

CHAPTER 17

Olivia pushed her way up to the front of the crowd. She smirked and asked loudly, "What were you thinking?"

Despite the feeling of wanting to hide, Julia managed to sit up straight. "I was thinking that the next time I go swimming, I'm going to beat all my personal best times!" She glared at Olivia.

"Oh, this is all about PBD." Olivia rolled her eyes. "Stuff happens. Sometimes you just have to wait."

At that moment, Julia felt as though Olivia might have a good, valid point. But she refused to admit it. Instead, Julia just pretended Olivia wasn't there.

Mom placed her hand on Julia's shoulder and nobody spoke.

"Why are they taking so long?" Julia asked Lorna.

Lorna looked up from her phone. "Patience, Julia. Patience. The art room is way at the other end of the center. And Ms. Fargas's supply closet is probably full of stuff she's got to sort through."

"Everybody is trying to help you," Mom reminded her.

Julia sighed. "Okay, Eomma, okay."

Even though it was hard, Julia sat on the stool and waited.

To keep herself busy, Julia counted how long it took her father to get a fresh sheet of seaweed, lay it out on the bamboo mat, add a layer of rice, and fill it before rolling it up tight. Forty-five seconds! His fingers flew. He worked quickly, but carefully.

Before she knew it, Ms. Fargas handed Lorna a white bottle of acetone. Julia wasn't sure what acetone was.

"What do you usually use this stuff for?" Julia asked Ms. Fargas.

"Removing sticky stuff." The corners of her eyes crinkled a tiny bit.

Julia's mood lifted. "I've definitely got a sticky stuff problem."

"You sure do!" Ms. Fargas agreed.

"Thank you!" Lorna said to Ms. Fargas. "We'll be sure to bring this back to you."

"Don't worry, I know where you work. I've got to get back to my job. You let me know what happens." Ms. Fargas pushed her cart down the hallway.

Julia wished, very silently, that Stevie would hurry up already! But she held her lips tightly together so that she would stay patient — or at least stay quiet about it.

"Excuse me!" Stevie said loudly, weaving in and out of the crowd of people.

She held a bag of cotton balls high above her head.

Finally! Julia was thrilled to see her.

"Sorry, sorry!" she said breathlessly. "I've really got to organize that room!" She handed Lorna the bag.

"I'm going to soak a few cotton balls. Will you help me?" Lorna asked Julia's mother.

Mom nodded.

Lorna put a few cotton balls at the open mouth of the acetone bottle and flipped it over for a few seconds. She handed Julia's mother the wet balls. "Try to soak the skin where the glue is touching."

"Okay," Mom said, suddenly looking very serious.

The balls smelled weird. Not bad, Julia thought, just weird. But mostly, they were cold at first. Then, after a few seconds, they warmed up.

She scrunched her face.

"Stay still," Mom ordered.

Lorna continued to soak cotton balls with acetone. Then she held them up to the part of her jaw that Mom hadn't soaked yet.

Julia felt some liquid dripping down her chin and onto her neck, but she did not say anything. She dabbed at her neck with the wet towel and tried not to think about all the hands around her head.

"How long do you think?" Mom asked Lorna, still looking concerned.

"Let's make sure the skin is good and wet."

From where she sat, through the glass wall behind the sushi café, Julia could see the giant pace clock in the aquatic center. It had colored hands that didn't actually tell the time. It was used to keep track of lap times. Julia watched the red hand sweep past the sixty-second marker, and she counted as it went around and around three times. One hundred and eighty-seconds. Three minutes. She could swim a lot of laps in that time.

When she was swimming, three minutes could pass so quickly. When she was sitting on a stool with stinky cotton balls pressed up against the side of her face, three minutes felt like almost forever.

Julia's mother and Lorna glanced at each other, unsure what to do next.

Lorna put down her cotton ball. "Well?" she asked Mom.

Mom shrugged her shoulders and then began to pick at the rim of the bowl with her fingernail.

Julia felt something! Like a tiny little pop.

Lorna looked excited. "Did it just come apart?" She peered at the side of Julia's face.

"Yes!" Mom said.

The crowd in front of the café's counter surged forward. Dad had given up making rolls.

Julia couldn't take her eyes off her mother, who had crouched down to get a better view.

"Maybe new cotton balls?" Mom suggested.

Lorna immediately soaked fresh balls and applied them to Julia's face while Mom carefully started to push Julia's skin while gently pulling at the bowl.

The fresh acetone dribbled down Julia's neck like a tiny little stream. But she didn't dare move and she let the liquid run instead of wiping it up.

Mom kept picking around the edge of the bowl. Another little pop. The crowd of spectators gasped.

Lorna kept pressing a moist ball up against Julia's jaw and cheek. Julia's mother worked carefully and precisely. Another little pop.

"Oh, my goodness!" Stevie proclaimed. "This is surprisingly nerve-racking!"

When the bowl finally pulled away from the skin under Julia's jaw, a small cheer erupted from the crowd.

Mom and Lorna both leapt for joy and hugged each other.

Julia was so relieved, she slid off the stool and started to jump for joy with them. That's when the bowl smacked her in the nose. It was off her skin, but the bowl was still stuck to her hair.

CHAPTER 18

"Ouch!" Julia rubbed her nose. "Now what?" The container dangled in the air.

"I think we'll have to cut your hair," Mom said. She lifted the bowl to see how much hair was stuck to it.

Everybody fell silent for a few moments before Dad said loudly, "It will be a bowl cut." He brought his fist up to his mouth and hid a laugh. A few people standing around the counter chuckled.

"That's *not* funny," Julia told him, annoyed.

Mom turned around and her shoulders started to shake. Julia sometimes wished her parents had never learned to tell jokes in English.

"Well, I have to get back to the reference desk," Lorna said with a smile. She stretched out her back.

"We are grateful for your research," Dad said.

Mom held out her hands to Lorna. Lorna grasped them. "How can we thank you?"

"Just make sure you keep on giving me the biggest pieces of tofu in the pot." Lorna winked.

"Always." Mom smiled.

"Thank you, Lorna," Julia said. She rubbed the skin where the bowl had been stuck. It felt a little tingly. The bowl still pulled painfully at her hair.

"Let's *stick* to things like reading for the next little while, okay?" Lorna said, holding back a smile.

Julia didn't like Lorna's jokes in English either.

"I guess it's only five more days," Julia said quietly.

"That's right," Lorna agreed. "Your next chance to go to a swim meet will come up soon. You'll be even *better* and *faster* then, I promise." Lorna leaned in and whispered, "Remember, you don't have to *miss* PBD. You could still participate, but maybe not in the way you expected to." She waved goodbye to the Nam family and left.

Julia felt confused by what Lorna had just said.

How could she participate in PBD? She wasn't allowed to swim! It was as if Lorna had completely misunderstood the whole bowl glued to the side of Julia's head situation!

She brooded on Lorna's parting words for a few moments. *Participate in PBD — I wish!*

Now that the excitement had calmed down, the crowd started to thin out. Dad resumed pressing rolls and Julia's mother started to tidy up the small pile of cotton balls and wet towels.

Julia was gently tapping the bowl still dangling from her hair.

"Where are those scissors?" Mom asked. She lightly rubbed Julia's cheek before starting her hunt for the scissors, which always seemed to end up in unexpected places.

Scissors. Her mother was going to have to cut the bowl away from her hair, right now, right here. There was no other way.

Julia pulled at a few strands, but her hair would not come loose. This glue sure was good. Too good.

Before her mother was able to find the scissors, she got distracted with a customer at the counter. Mom held up a finger so that Julia knew to wait.

Julia felt as if she was becoming an expert at waiting.

She sighed and got as cozy as she could

on her stool. The sights of the community center were familiar and comforting: people walking by carrying hockey bags, teens with their backpacks, parents staring at their cell-phones, young children holding books from the library, and there was always at least one baby crying.

"Eomma. Scissors," Julia reminded her mother when the customer left.

Her mother turned quickly. "Uh? Oh, sorry, sorry." She lifted a small pile of paper bags and then a towel before finally finding what she was looking for.

Julia was sure that those scissors had been used to cut things like fish cakes, or even onions. Mom gave them a quick wash before tucking them into the front pocket of her apron.

Mom motioned for Julia to go to an empty table near the café.

As Julia walked, the bowl swayed, like a clock pendulum, against her head.

Mom stood next to her and held the

scissor tips near the dangling bowl. Just before she started to cut, she said, "You surprise me."

"In a good way or a bad way?" Julia asked, worried.

Mom looked up, searching for what she wanted to say. "A surprise can be both. Bad thing, you need a haircut from *me*. But it's only hair. Good thing, you show your heart."

"My heart?" Julia asked, confused.

Mom looked up again. "Maybe not the right word." She quickly ducked under the counter and took a peek at Dad's weekly vocabulary list before returning. "Maybe

I mean, you showed me . . ." Mom paused, "your *devotion*."

Julia thought about what her mother had said. She added, "When something is important, you will do anything for it. Even . . ." Julia glanced at the bottle of acetone on the counter a few feet away, "maybe weird things."

Julia and her mother burst into laughter.

"So, if swimming is so important to you, maybe you can go to the pool next time and sit inside, maybe just watch?" Mom jerked her head in the direction of the pool.

"Why would I do that? Won't I feel worse?"

"Can you feel *worse*?" Mom asked in disbelief.

"No, I guess I couldn't . . ."

"Maybe you have to *roll* with it." From behind the counter, Dad waved an uncut sushi roll in the air like a baton. He started chuckling.

Saleema had said the same thing about "rolling" with it, but because she wasn't waving a California roll at the time, it hadn't sounded so corny. "*Appa* . . ." Julia moaned at her father's joke.

Then she remembered something. "Lorna said I should turn PBD into *T*BD, Team Best Day, but . . ."

Julia became lost in thought, so she didn't really notice when her mother chopped the bowl off her hair.

CHAPTER 19

Julia tucked her short hair behind her ears. She still wasn't used to it because it had only been a few days. The haircut her mother had given her was a little uneven, but she had done her best. Mom promised Julia that they would go to a proper hair salon on the weekend.

"Julia!" Coach Marissa said. "Hold this!"

Julia bent over and helped Coach attach the electronic timing pad to lane two. Olivia's usual lane.

Julia didn't think much about it. She

didn't have time to think. There was a lot to set up during Personal Best Day.

Just as Julia was helping Coach finish setting up the last timing pad in lane three, Coach gave her a long look and smiled.

Julia felt embarrassed. "Why are you looking at me like that?"

"I like your hair," Coach said. "It's kind of choppy."

"That's because my mother doesn't know how to cut hair."

"I meant choppy in a good way," Coach said, laughing.

"Oh. Thanks, I guess."

Coach got up off her knees and stretched her back. "Okay, can you get the whiteboard?"

Julia hopped up and ran over to the wheeled board and pushed it closer to the lanes, while Coach tested the timers.

"Oh, before practice starts, make sure you put this on." Coach held something out to her.

Julia looked at it — a whistle! The fabric of the lanyard was decorated with the Vipers logo. It looked just like the one Coach had.

"Take it," Coach said, shaking the whistle in her hand. A small plastic card, attached to the lanyard with a metal loop swung loose.

Reluctantly, Julia reached for it.

"Look at the card," Coach said. It had a small photo of Julia and looked something like an ID card. On the bottom it said: *JULIA NAM: Doing my PB all day long.*

"I know you're disappointed about today. But as your coach, I'm proud of you for coming out and supporting your teammates."

"How'd you know I would come and help today?" Julia asked, admiring her personalized ID card and whistle.

"Just a hunch. I think a lot of swimmers think they are swimming by themselves, and maybe even *for* themselves, but actually, we're a swim *team*, aren't we? We all want our own best times, that's for sure, so we push each

other to do better. But we also support each other at the same time, right?"

"I'm a Viper," Julia said. "I'll be able to swim PBD next time." She looked up to meet Coach's eyes. "But right now, I've just got to roll with it."

"What are you two talking about?" Olivia had come out of the changeroom and stood right beside Julia. Other members started to come onto the pool deck too.

Julia slipped the lanyard over her head. "Oh, just Vipers stuff."

"What does *that* mean?" Olivia asked.

"That means you'd better swim your best today, because the next time we do PBD, you know I'm going to swim mine."

Julia put the whistle in her mouth and blew. The sound echoed around the aquatic center loud and clear. She tucked her short hair behind her ears and got ready to cheer on her team.

ACKNOWLEDGMENTS

I thought about this book for a long time. Many things about the story changed over time, but at the core of it, it always involved an immigrant family running a sushi restaurant — that was the one constant.
I didn't know too much about running a sushi restaurant, but I happen to live in the most sushi-obsessed city outside of Japan, so there was no shortage of places to conduct research. Luckily, while doing my due diligence, I also happened to be able to order lunch. I love multitasking.

Thank you to all the small family-run restaurants who feed us.

I did know a thing or two about swimming, though. My daughter has been swimming regularly for more than a decade. I will brag that she finished her Red Cross Level 10 at the age of nine. (In Canada, the Red Cross swim programs have been phased out in favor of the Swim For Life program.) Twenty-two swimsuits, nineteen goggles, and seven swim caps later, my daughter is still swimming (with a non-competitive group). She is the reason I came up with the character of Julia.

The people who helped me get this book in your hands remains a small, tight group. Thank you to my beta reader, Kyla Z., and to my family, who patiently listened to me while I brainstormed ideas at the dinner table. (While marveling at my own thoughts, I may have also made several claims about my own brilliance.) There are two special people I work with who help me behind the scenes: my agent,

Laurel Symonds, and my editor, Lynne
Missen. I cannot imagine doing a book
without you two. Thank you endlessly.

For the utterly charming cover and
interior illustrations, I will always be indebted
to Julie Kim and the art direction of the
Tundra team.

Lastly, the Hillcrest Community Centre
was the inspiration for the setting of this story.
Located in the heart of Vancouver, it is also
the heart of this book. (Is it weird to thank a
building? Too bad, I'm doing it.) Many thanks
to the Hillcrest Community Centre for giving
Julia Nam her second home.